Café Kichijouji de 2

ORIGINAL CONCEPT BY
Yuki MIYAMOTO

TABLE OF CONTENTS

Translation	Sachiko Sato
Lettering	Studio Cutie
Graphic Design	Eric Rosenberger
Editing	Stephanie Donnelly
Editor in Chief	Fred Lui
Publisher	Hikaru Sasahara

English Edition Published by
DIGITAL MANGA PUBLISHING
A division of DIGITAL MANGA, Inc.
1487 W 178th Street, Suite 300
Gardena, CA 90248

www.dmpbooks.com

First Edition: January 2006
ISBN: 1-56970-948-3

1 3 5 7 9 10 8 6 4 2

Printed in China

Café Kichijouji de
COLOR SPECIAL
OH?
ARE YOU GROWING A MUSTACHE TOO, BOSS?
WHA...

...AND THAT...
...WAS THE NEW YEAR'S DREAM I HAD.
WOW!
IT WAS LIKE A BAD OMEN TELLING ME NOTHING GOOD WOULD COME OF MY GROWING A MUSTACHE...
IT WAS JUST A DREAM. YOU'RE TAKING IT TOO SERIOUSLY!
HE'S RIGHT. IT SUITS YOU.
THE CONSOLERS.
...LOOKING SO *GEEZER-ISH* AND ALL.
GEEZER...!
A MUSTACHE, HUH?
MAYBE I'LL GROW ONE, TOO.
THE RAZOR'S SO ABRASIVE DURING THE WINTER. IT HURTS MY FACE.
MY SKIN GETS SO DRY...
I KNOW WHAT YOU MEAN.
JUST THE OTHER DAY, I WAS SHAVING WITH THE BOX CUTTER AND BLOODIED MYSELF ALL OVER...
THE BLADE IS TOO WOBBLY ON THOSE THINGS!
THAT'S NOT QUITE THE SAME THING...
I UNDERSTAND.

IN RECOGNITION OF YOUR LOOK, OUR STORE WILL NOW REIGN OVER THIS LAND AS THE NEW "MUSTACHE CAFÉ"!
WHAT THE...
HA HA HA HA HA HA
EVERYONE BE SURE TO GROW A MUSTACHE BY TOMORROW!
STOP MESSING WITH MY SHOP'S ORIGINAL BUSINESS PLAN...
CAFÉ DE MUSTACHE
WHAT ARE YOU SAYING? THIS IS ALL BECAUSE I HAVE A COMPLETE UNDERSTANDING OF YOUR BUSINESS PHILOSOPHY!
WE ARE BROTHERS-IN-MUSTACHES!
DON'T YOU MEAN A WARPED UNDERSTANDING...?
ISN'T THIS OUT OF CHARACTER FOR YOU?
DON'T BE UNREASONABLE, MINAGAWA!
IT TAKES ME AN ENTIRE WEEK TO GROW A PROPER MUSTACHE.
BY TOMORROW IS IMPOSSIBLE!
THAT'S WHAT HE'S OBJECTING TO...?!
TSK TSK!
TARO...YOU MUST HAVE A NUTRITIONAL DEFICIENCY OR SOMETHING.
WITH A PROPERLY BALANCED DIET, YOU CAN INSTANTLY GROW ONE A GOOD TWO METERS LONG...
NO, YOU COULDN'T!
MACKEREL IN MISO WORKS WELL.
OH, NO WONDER...

IT JUST WON'T STOP GROWING THIS MORNING...
ISN'T IT A BIT LATE FOR A "GUNDAM TURN A" MUSTACHE?
MY MUS-TACHE.
I HAD SABAMISO FOR BREAKFAST, SO...
HUH! はっ
びくっ HA!
WHA?
2002 1月 2
CHIRP ちゅん CHIRP ちゅん
OH? YOU SHAVED OFF YOUR MUSTACHE?
I CHANGED MY MIND...
BUT YOU WERE SO CHILDISHLY STUBBORN ABOUT CHANGING YOUR IMAGE OVER THE HOLIDAYS THIS YEAR AND SURPRISING YOUR STAFF...
A NEW YEAR'S DREAM GIM-MICK.

第6話
Chapter

YEAH, AND THE CHERRY BLOSSOMS AT THE PARK ARE AWESOME!
THERE'RE EVEN PEOPLE OUT FLOWER-VIEWING...
BY TOMORROW, THEY'LL BE IN FULL BLOOM, I BET.
IT'S LIKE, WHOOOA!
HUH...

CAN'T WE PLAN TO DO SOMETHING LIKE THAT?
YOU MEAN FLOWER-VIEWING?
LET'S DO IT! WE'LL MAKE BOXED LUNCHES...
YOU'RE RIGHT...
IT MIGHT BE NICE TO TAKE IN THE SEASONS...
I PASS.
OUTINGS LIKE THOSE ARE JUST WAY TOO MUCH TROUBLE.
I AGREE.
EVEN YOU, MR. TARO...
THUMP!
I DON'T FEEL LIKE HANGING OUT WITH THE SAME OL' FACES EVEN ON MY DAY OFF.
ALL THAT ASIDE...

...HOW IS IT THAT YOU KNOW SO MUCH ABOUT THE PARK WHEN IT'S NOWHERE NEAR YOUR SHOPPING ROUTE?
THE WEATHER'S REALLY NICE, AND NOBODY WOULD KNOW IF WE JUST TOOK A LITTLE DETOUR...
...IS WHAT MR. TOKU SAID.
GAAH!
JUN...!
ONE MUST DECLARE ONE'S INNO-CENCE.
CANDID
BEING INFLU-ENCED BY MAKI IN SUCH TRIVIAL WAYS...
PAR-DON?
DID YOU SAY SOME-THING, LITTLE TARO?
SO, NOT ONLY IS YOUR BRAIN GONE, BUT YOUR HEAR-ING AS WELL...
DON'T COMPARE ME TO YOU, YOU YOUNG GEEZER!
WHO'S A GEEZER?! I'M ONLY A YEAR OLDER THAN YOU!
WHAT SHALL WE DO?
...FOR-GET IT.

SO...
CLOSED FOR THE DAY
ABOUT RESERVING A SPACE FOR TOMORROW'S FLOWER-VIEWING...
OH? ARE WE GOING FLOWER-VIEWING AFTER ALL?!
WE ARE.
HOLD ON A SECOND.
LIKE I SAID BEFORE...
THE BOSS...
...HE WAS LOOKING SO GLOOMY AS HE GAZED LONGINGLY AT A TOUR GUIDE PAMPHLET TITLED: *"SPRINGTIME! THE CHERRY BLOSSOM TRAVEL TOUR GUIDE"...*
I KNOW - I'LL GO TO KYOTO...
DUDE...

WELL... IF THAT'S THE CASE...
YAAAAY!
THEN USING THIS FOURTH-DIMENSIONAL AMIDA CHART...
START!!
OH ALL RIGHT, ALL RIGHT!!
WE NEED TO DECIDE WHO GOES TO RESERVE A SPACE, RIGHT?
ROCK-PAPER-SCISSORS! ONE SHOT ONLY! IF YOU DON'T PUT YOUR HAND OUT, YOU LOSE!
THE FIRST ONE'S A
ROCK...!
OK, IT'S DECIDED...
YOUR SHALLOW TACTICS ARE SO EASY TO SEE THROUGH.

WHA...
WHAT IS IT, MR. MAKI?!
EEK!
GRAB
LET'S HAVE A NICE, LONG TALK THROUGH-OUT THE NIGHT...
WHY ME?!
HERE'S A MAT.
BUT WON'T IT BE TOUGH TO SAVE A SPACE AT THE PARK AT THIS LATE HOUR?
THE GOOD SPOTS WILL PROBABLY BE TAKEN ALREADY.
IT'S OKAY...

I KNOW A GOOD SPACE...
DOOOOM
......
WE'RE SUPPOSED TO SPEND THE NIGHT HERE...?!
MR. MAKI, THIS WAY, *THIS WAY!*

WOW...
THIS IS A PRIME SPOT, FOR SURE.
IT'S AMAZING MR. MINAGAWA KNEW OF SUCH A PLACE!
HE'S ODDLY WELL-INFORMED ABOUT THE *STRANGEST* THINGS...
IS IT OKAY TO PUT THE MAT RIGHT ABOUT HERE?
FLAP
TOKU...

SO LONG!
I LEAVE THE REST TO YOU!
WHA...
WHIRL...
HUH? WHAT?!
W-WAIT A MINUTE!
I'M SUPPOSED TO STAY IN THIS CREEPY PLACE ALL BY MYSELF?!
GRAB
IT'S FOR THE BOSS! SUCK IT UP!
YOU'RE HEARTLESS, MR. MAKI!!

SHUT UP! BE A MAN AND JUST...
AND JUST WHAT?!
CLANK!
?!
WHAT?
DID YOU... HEAR SOMETHING JUST NOW...?
I DON'T HEAR ANYTHING.
DON'T CREEP ME OUT.
BUT... I'M SURE I JUST HEARD...
...THE SOUND OF A HAMMER HITTING SOME-THING...
CLANK

CLANK
MI...!
FLINCH
HA!
WHAT ARE YOU DOING, MR. MINAGAWA?!
I WAS WORRIED WHETHER YOU GOT HERE OKAY.
WE'RE TALKING ABOUT THAT THING IN YOUR HAND...

*Note: "Isn't it nice not to be alone" is a lyric from an old song by Mari Amachi.

WHAT'S EVERYONE DOING HERE?
GOOD EVENING!
MR. MINAGAWA SAID IT WOULD BE FUN TO SWING BY... AND BRING YOU SOME FOOD.
HERE!
FOOD?! REALLY?!
THUD
WOW...
IT SURE IS A BEAUTIFUL SIGHT...
IF YOU DON'T LOOK AROUND BACK, THAT IS.
CHERRY BLOS-SOMS...

WHEN THEY'RE PLANTED, YOU'RE SUPPOSED TO BURY A CORPSE AT THE ROOTS, RIGHT?
BFFT!
THAT'S SERIOUSLY UNTRUE.
BUT I THOUGHT THAT MAKES THE GROUND MORE FERTILE...
THEN THAT WOULD MEAN SCHOOLS ARE BUILT ON HUGE GRAVE-YARDS!!
BUT COME TO THINK OF IT...
...WE USED TO HAVE A BIG PERSIMMON TREE AT OUR HOUSE.
WHEN MY PET DOG DIED, I BURIED HIM UNDER THAT TREE.
THEN...
...THAT TREE, WHICH HAD NEVER PUT FORTH A SINGLE FRUIT BEFORE...
BEGAN TO PRODUCE BIG PERSIMMONS THE FOLLOWING YEAR...
GOGOGO
BLAAAH!
BLOS-SOMS...

FURIOUSLY THEY BLOOM, ALL THE MORE BEAUTIFULLY AS THEY FEED ON A HUMAN'S GRUDGING FLESH...
CUT IT OUT!
OH, THERE'S THIS INCIDENT THAT REALLY HAPPENED AT SCHOOL...
I SAID CUT IT OUT!!
WHAT ARE YOU SO MAD ABOUT?
YOU GUYS CAN SAY ALL YOU WANT BECAUSE YOU GET TO GO HOME.
BUT I HAVE TO STAY HERE ALL NIGHT!
THAT'S WHY WE THOUGHT THE LEAST WE COULD DO WAS BRING YOU SOME FOOD...
ODEN AND OTHER STUFF...
THEY'RE JUST BOX LUNCHES FROM THE CONVENIENCE STORE!
IF YOU REALLY CARE, THEN TRADE PLACES WITH ME!
OH.
I ALMOST FORGOT.
G
PAY UP.
↑RECEIPT

DAMMIT!
DON'T USE THIS AS AN EXCUSE TO LEAVE!
NOW NOW...
CLANK
FLOP!
IT'S SUCH A GOOD SPOT, BUT WITH MR. MAKI IN THAT CONDITION...
HOLD HIM DOWN
SOB SOB
YOU'RE RIGHT...
THEN...
KEEP OUT
SUHUH

CLONK
FINISHED...
TO HE WHO TRESPASSES AGAINST MY WILL, THE WINGS OF DEATH SHALL DESCEND UPON THEE.
KEEP
THUNK
WITH SUCH HIGHLY SUSPICIOUS MARKINGS, NO ONE WILL DARE TO COME NEAR.
IS THAT THE INTENDED EFFECT?
A SARDINE HEAD...
KEEP
BUMP
SO NOW WE CAN GO HOME, RIGHT?
ALLEY-OOP!

ZAP
KA-THUD
WHAT HAPPENED?
IT'S LIKE I WAS BOUNCED BACK...
OH, COME ON...
?
HUH...?
IT'S TRUE, I TELL YOU.
ZAP!
AAAGGGHH!!
THUD
SO IMMATURE...

MR. MAKI ...!
HEY, MINA-GAWA!
WHAT'S GOING ON...?
IT SEEMS THE AFFECTED TARGETS ARE SPECIFIC.
MRGH...
KEEP OUT
?!
ZAP

WH...
WHAT'S WRONG? I THOUGHT YOU COULD PASS THROUGH?
HMPH!
GLARE
ULP!
MINA-GAWA--!!
WHY AM I TREATED JUST LIKE THEM?!
THAT'S YOUR MAIN COM-PLAINT?
THE DIRECTIONAL EFFECT SEEMS TO HAVE CHANGED...
HUH?
IN OTHER WORDS, THE SPIRITUAL INTENSITY AMPLIFIED BY THIS SARDINE'S HEAD HAS PRODUCED A SIDE-EFFECT, CAUSING THE POWER ORIGINALLY INTENDED TO GENERATE IN A BI-DIRECTIONAL PATTERN TO OVERLOAD BY PRODUCING THREE-TIMES THE NORMAL RESISTANCE, THUS...
UHH...
CAN YOU MAKE THAT EASIER TO UNDER-STAND...?

THE GIST IS THAT I MESSED UP.
DOES THAT MEAN WE'LL NEVER BE ABLE TO GET OUT OF HERE?
NOT RIGHT AWAY, NO.
BUT I GOT OUT JUST FINE.
UH, NO...
I THINK YOU'RE AN EXCEPTION ON THE ATOMIC STRUCTURE-LEVEL.
WE'LL COME GET YOU TOMORROW.
GOOD-BYE.
WHA...
ARE YOU SERIOUS?!
HMM!

YESTER-DAY, 10 P.M.
SUKEKIYO AND HIS FRIENDS DID AN EXCELLENT JOB.
IT MUST'VE BEEN HARD TO RESERVE SUCH A GOOD SPOT AT THE PARK.
NOT AT ALL.
I HAD A BACKUP LOCATION RESERVED...
...BUT THAT'S ANOTHER STORY...
ARE TARO AND THE OTHERS NOT COMING, THEN?
NO...
OH, WELL...THEY WEREN'T SO BIG ON THE IDEA ANYWAY.
AND IT'S NICE TO BE ABLE TO HAVE A CALM, QUIET DAY OFF FOR ONCE.

GOOD TO KNOW.
OH...
?
IT WAS WORTH ALL THE PREPARATION TO HEAR YOU SAY THAT.
NOW I SEE...
MURMUR
ARE THEY DEAD?
AND THEY'RE SO YOUNG...
MURMUR
ZZZZ
UNDER THESE BLUE SKIES...BASED ON THE REPORT OF LOCAL RESIDENTS, THE LAW IS ABOUT TO BE ENFORCED...20 SECONDS AND COUNTING.

Tiny
Café Kichijouji de
第6話
Chapter
ZA-...
It's been raining for over a week now.
It's true.

Even though we're making all these Teruteru dolls...
It's not letting up at all.
They say when you throw a sandal and it lands right-side-up, the weather will be fair, and if it lands upside-down, it'll rain.
So that means if all of us manage to throw right-side-up...
I know! Let's figure out tomorrow's weather ourselves!
Huh?

Then tomorrow will be fair, no question!
Then let's get started...
PATA
PATA
Come on, weather! Tomorrow be fair!

....
....
After this, the rain continued for an entire month.
ZAAAZ...
....

第7話 Chapter

UGH... THAT TOOK WAY TOO LONG.
JUST TO EXCHANGE MONEY!
THIS IS WHY I HATE GOING TO THE BANK AT NOON...
GRIP

HUH?
PAPA...
SOB!
WHAT?!
WAAAAAH!
NOISY KID...
WHO ARE YOU CALLING "PAPA"?!
WHAT A HORRID PARENT!
NOOO!
PAPA!!
STOP CLINGING TO ME!
OH, DEAR.
I'M NOT YOUR PAPA!
PAPAAAAA!!
WHO ARE YOU, CHIBI-MARU?!
...YES.
PLEASE WAIT ONE MOMENT.

MAKI, WHERE'S THE BOSS?
WHAT ARE YOU DOING UP THERE?!
WHAT DOES IT MATTER?
BOSS, TELEPHO--
WIPE WIPE
WIPE WIPE
BOSS?
B--
HUH?
STOP
STARE
YES, THIS IS HE...
IS HE OKAY?
WHAT DO YOU MEAN?
THE BOSS... IT'S LIKE HE'S BEEN DRAINED OF LIFE.

WELL, THE SHOP'S BEEN PRETTY BUSY...
I DON'T THINK HE'S EVEN BEEN ABLE TO GET HOME MUCH LATELY.
IT'S NO WONDER...
IS THAT RIGHT?
AND TOKU ALWAYS GETS THE ORDERS WRONG, JUN BASHES HOLES IN EVERYTHING, TARO IS VIOLENT, AND YOU'RE ALWAYS GETTING DUMPED, MAKI.
THAT LAST ONE'S IRREL-EVANT!
WHAT?!
YES.
YES.
I'LL BE THERE RIGHT AWAY.
NO, NOT AT ALL...
YES.
MAKI, MINA-GAWA.
PIP!
YEAH...
I'M GOING OUT FOR A BIT.
I'M SORRY, BUT YOU TWO WILL HAVE TO STAY ON YOUR OWN FOR A WHILE.
HUH?
BUT TARO SHOULD BE COMING BACK SOON, RIGHT?
WAIT A MINUTE.

JUST THE TWO OF US? THAT'S IMPOSSIBLE (WITH MINAGAWA) ...!
I'M COUNTING ON YOU!
BOSS?!
WOW. HE MUST REALLY BE STRESSED-OUT TO LEAVE YOU IN CHARGE OF THE STORE, MAKI.
OH, WELL...
SEEING AS I'VE BEEN ENTRUSTED, I MIGHT AS WELL...
...MAKE A TIMELY CLOSURE OF THE STORE.
WE ARE CLOSED FOR TODAY. SEE YOU TOMORROW.
I SEE.
YOU'RE LATE, TARO.
UH, YEAH...
I RAN INTO A LITTLE...
A LITTLE ...?

YOU MEAN THIS?
SO, THIS IS HOW YOUR TASTES RUN, TARO!
YOU SHOULD TAKE HER BACK BEFORE THIS BECOMES A FELONY.
YOU PERVERT!
SHE FOLLOWED ME ON HER OWN!
I TRIED REPEATEDLY TO SHAKE HER ALONG THE WAY, BUT...
WHAT ARE YOU, EVIL?
SHE'S PERSISTENT...
SHE MUST BE LOST.
I GUESS WE SHOULD CALL THE POLICE AND HAVE THEM TAKE CARE OF HER...
WHAT'S YOUR NAME?
I'M NOT!

REINA ISN'T LOST!
PAPA?
REINA CAME TO SEE PAPA!
SO, I DON'T HAVE TO GO SEE THE POLICE-MAN!
TARO...
YOU SHOULD TAKE RESPON-SIBILITY FOR YOUR MISTAKES...
AT LEAST ACKNOWL-EDGE HER AS YOUR OWN...FOR THE KID'S SAKE!
HOW DID YOU COME TO THAT CONCLUSION?!
HEY, WHO IS YOUR PAPA?
THIS.
DON'T POINT!
I TOLD YOU I'M NOT!

HE HAS CLOTHES LIKE THIS.
OH, YOU FOLLOWED THE UNIFORM!
SO, IT REALLY IS SOMEBODY AT OUR STORE?
THEN CAN YOU TELL US YOUR PAPA'S NAME?
...
WHAT'S WRONG?
...PEE-PEE...
W.C.
FLUSH
WHAT ARE YOU GONNA DO ABOUT YOUR DAUGHTER?
CUT IT OUT.
WHEN MY HANDS ARE FREE, I'LL TAKE HER DOWN TO THE POLICE STATION...
OH, MY...! WHAT'S THIS?!

IS SOME-
THING
THE
MATTER?
JUST
LOOK
AT THIS
MESS!
ぐじゃ…
GLOP...
WHAT
THE...!
UGH...
AAHHH!!
NOOO!
あああああ
AAAHHHHH
WHAT'S
WITH
THIS
GIRL?!
STOP!
キャ
HEY!
WHAT DO
YOU
THINK
YOU'RE
DOING?!
THAT'S
THE
BATH-
ROOM
HOSE!

WAS IT YOU THAT MESSED UP THE TOILE--
BLURGH!
SPLOOSH
DRIBBLE DRIBBLE
NYAH!
ARRRGGGGGHHHH!!
BOW BOW
DDDDDDDD
YOU'RE NOT GETTING AWAY!!
TA TA TA TA
CLACK

THUD
BANG
CLANK
BONK
THUNK
CLATTER
PRACTICING A COMEDY ROUTINE?
YOU'RE IN THE WAY. DO IT SOMEWHERE ELSE.
AS IF!!
WHERE IS SHE?!
YOU MEAN LITTLE REINA?
PIP PIP
CLATTER CLATTER
SHE'S RIGHT BEHIND YOU...
DUMP
MAKI! WHAT ARE YOU DOING?!
HURRY UP AND TAKE CARE OF THE TOILE--
GOTCHA!!
KOFF KOFF
WHACK
WHOA!!

WHY ARE YOU THE ONE ON A RAMPAGE?!
SMASH
SMAASH!
TOSS ぽい
WOULDN'T IT BE BETTER TO CLOSE THE STORE TEMPORARILY?
SHUT UP, GIRLY-MAN!
WHO'S A GIRLY-MAN?!
CUT IT OUT, YOU LITTLE BRAT!
NYAAAH...
CRASH
TINKLE
AH, NOW I UNDERSTAND EXACTLY HOW THE BOSS FEELS.
I GUESS YOU'RE RIGHT...
HOWDY...
HUH? IT'S OPEN...
THAT'S STRANGE... IT'S ONLY CLOSED OUT FRONT.
TOKU!!

HER! CATCH HER!!
HUH?
TORO TORO TORO
JUST DO IT!
O...
OKAY!
BONK
A KITTY!
MEOW
!!
TOKU, DON'T LET HER GET AWAY!!
OWWW...
RIGHT!
THAT GIRL... COULD SHE BE...?
YOU KNOW HER?!

NO, I WAS JUST GUESSING SHE WAS THE ONE WHO DID THIS...
I THOUGHT IT WAS AN AWFULLY RETRO PRANK.
JUST WHAT KIND OF GRUDGE DOES SHE HAVE AGAINST THIS STORE?
DAMN! SO SHE EVEN GOT INTO THE LOCKERS!
WHOSE IS SHE?
JUN, IS THERE ANY CHANCE SHE MIGHT BE YOUR--
CLANG
?
LUNGE
GRAB
GOTCHA!

TIME TO SNIP YOUR LONG, LONG WHISKERS--
AAAAAHHH!!
CHK CHK
NO NO! DON'T CUT THE WHISKERS OFF!
NOOO!! REINA WANTS TO CUT THEM!!
HE WON'T CATCH MICE ANYMORE!
ANTIQUATED...
THAT'S ENOUGH.
I DON'T KNOW WHAT YOU'RE SO UNHAPPY ABOUT...
...BUT YOU STILL KNOW THE DIFFERENCE BETWEEN WHAT'S GOOD...
...AND WHAT'S BAD. DON'T YOU?
FLINCH

WHAT YOU JUST TRIED TO DO, REINA... WHICH ONE IS IT?
EEK!
B- BAD...
THEN LET'S APOLOGIZE...
TO SUKE-KIYO.
TO THE CAT?!
... ...
I'M SORRY...
YOUR FATHER WILL BE HERE SOON.
REALLY?!
UNTIL THEN, YOU CAN PLAY WITH THIS.
ぽい
TOSS

YOU FOUND OUT WHO TO CONTACT?
TUG TUG
THIS...
IT WAS IN HER BASKET.
たんぽぽ
みたかれいな
DANDELION
REINA MITAKA
OH...A CONTACT BOOK.
I REMEMBER THOSE!
WAIT A MINUTE...
WHAT?
MITAKA... THAT NAME SOUNDS FAMILIAR...
OH!
MY HAIR!
REINA!!
BAM

OHHH! THE BOSS!!
THEY DON'T LOOK ANYTHING ALIKE.
ARE YOU SURE SHE'S NOT A GRAND-CHILD?!
NO WAY!
AND WHY SUCH A BAD TEMPER?!
IS SHE A BLACK SHEEP?
CARRY ME!
HUH? WHAT'S UP WITH YOU GUYS...?
PA-PA--
COME TO THINK OF IT, HE WAS THE MOST LIKELY CANDIDATE OF ALL...
IT NEVER EVEN OCCURRED TO ME...
YOU KNOW?
I DIDN'T KNOW THE OLD MAN WAS CAPABLE OF SUCH A RESPON-SIBILITY...
I WAS WORRIED... YOU RUNNING OFF FROM NURSERY SCHOOL LIKE THAT.
BUT...
...I WANTED TO SEE YOU, PAPA.
BECAUSE YOU NEVER COME HOME FROM THE STORE...

BUT IF THE STORE GOES "OUT OF BUSINESS" YOU CAN STAY AT HOME, RIGHT?
HER EYES ARE SERIOUS...
DON'T TELL ME...THAT DISASTER OUT THERE IS...
TUF TUF
WELL... YES.
I'M SORRY ABOUT MY DAUGHTER.
IT'S ALL RIGHT.
WE'LL TAKE CARE OF THE REST.
PLEASE STAY WITH HER FOR THE REST OF THE DAY.
I THINK SHE MISSED YOU A LOT.
TAKE SOME TIME OFF AND RELAX, BOSS.
RIGHT, RIGHT.
YOU GUYS...
I'M IN YOUR DEBT.
THANK YOU.
SOB!
YAWN
CLATTER CLATTER
JUST HURRY UP AND GET THAT LITTLE DEMON AWAY FROM HERE...

WHAT A HEART-WARMING STORY...*
BY THE WAY...
...IS NO ONE GOING TO TELL ME WHAT HAPPENED BEFORE I HAVE TO CLEAN UP THIS MESS?
DRAINED
DON'T ASK.
CLATTER CLATTER
* JUST HIS IMAGINATION.
THE NEXT DAY...
WHOA!
HEY! THE BOSS HASN'T RECOVERED AT ALL!
IN FACT, HE'S GOTTEN WORSE.
OH... ABOUT THAT...
YESTER-DAY...HIS DAUGH-TER...
BOSS
YOU KNOW WHAT...?

REINA...
REINA IS GOING TO MARRY MR. MINAGAWA!
...IS WHAT SHE SAID.
I SEE...
TO CHOOSE MINAGAWA, OF ALL PEOPLE...
DON'T WORRY, SIR. KIDS CHANGE THEIR MINDS ALL THE TIME.
Y-YOU'RE RIGHT.
HAHA!
YES, HE'S RIGHT.
FA-THER.
DON'T CALL ME FATHER-RR!!
BOSS, CALM DOWN.
GO GET THE ASPIRIN!
WHOA!
A HURRIED END!!

Tinyの第7話 Chapter

It's sooo hot!!
What's wrong? You look so frazzled.
The air-conditioner busted.
And a fan doesn't do any good in this heat, either...
Why are you okay?
It doesn't feel hot to me.
What?!

But it's 100°F today!
Yeah.
You're really okay?
Heater.
Dotera and Kotatsu.
DON!
and Nabeyaki udon.

Campfire...
GOO...
DERO
So you're really not hot at all, Mr. Minagawa?
It's just mind over matter.
Portable air-conditioner!

第8話 Chapter

ALTHOUGH THESE BOYS MAY BE ENGAGED IN DESTRUCTION MOST OF THE TIME...
HEY, WAIT...
...EVEN THEY ARE ENTITLED TO PROTECTION BY LAWS AND SUCH.
TOKU--
AND THOUGH IT MAY NOT SEEM TO MAKE BUSINESS SENSE...
THEY GET PAID.
STUFFED
HUH?!
SO THICK?!

WHAT IS THIS NEVER-BEFORE-SEEN THICK-NESS?!
ARE THEY ALL 1000-YEN BILLS?
TOKUMI
OR MAYBE IT'S COUPONS AS COMPENSATION...
EITHER WAY, THIS LOOKS GOOD!!
THE ALL-YOU-CAN-EAT BEEF BARBEQUE OF MY DREAMS!!
無煙ロースタ
炭火焼き肉喰べ放
お1人様 1980
制限時間 90分
SMOKELESS GRILL ALL-YOU-CAN-EAT CHARCOAL-GRILLED BARBEQUE BEEF
PER PERSON 1,980 YEN TIME LIMIT 90 MINUTES
じゅ
SIZZLE
FOR ONE AS POVERTY-STRICKEN AS HE, A MEAL COSTING OVER 1,000 YEN WAS UNTHINKABLE UNLESS IT WAS ON THE BON FESTIVAL (LANTERN FESTIVAL) OR NEW YEAR'S.
PLEASE DON'T ADD SUCH A WEIRD NARRATION.
I WOULDN'T IF I WERE YOU. EATING EXPENSIVE FOOD YOU'RE NOT USED TO WILL ONLY MAKE YOU SICK.
STICK TO THE REGULAR 280 YEN MEAL.
WHY SHOULDN'T I?
YOU MIGHT WANT TO START BY FINISHING OFF THE OLDER FOOD FIRST...LIKE YOUR EMERGENCY RATIONS.
TOKU'S FOOD RESERVE
I TOLD YOU, THEY'RE NOT FOR FOOD...
OH!
GONE
FLAP
YOU REALLY GOT THAT MUCH?
YOU'RE JUST A PART-TIMER.

ちゃりーん
KA-CHING
KARAOKE COUPONS
TWO-HUNDRED AND EIGHT YEN...
LAST MONTH YOU AT LEAST STILL HAD SOME GREEN BILLS INSIDE.
HOW DOES THIS GUY KNOW THE CONTENTS OF OTHER PEOPLE'S PAY ENVELOPES ...?
A PATENT DISREGARD OF BASIC LABOR LAWS...
THAT'S 1.5 YEN AN HOUR.

SOB
BOSS!
UH... THERE'S A REASON FOR THIS...
TOKU.
LAST MONTH YOU BROKE THE DISH-WASHER, DIDN'T YOU?
THUD
HUH...? BUT I THOUGHT THAT WAS STILL COVERED BY THE WARRANTY...
THE MACHINE, YES.
BUT THE THINGS THAT WERE INSIDE IT ARE ANOTHER MATTER!
11 GLASSES, 6 SETS OF TEACUPS, 4 SETS OF COFFEE CUPS, 1 TEAPOT AND 2 LARGE PLATES!
8 SMALL PLATES AND VARIOUS PIECES OF CUTLERY, 27 IN ALL!
ETC., ETC.
WITH THESE DAMAGES DEDUCTED, THAT IS THE AMOUNT OF YOUR RESULTING PAY!
AND HOW MANY TIMES HAVE I TOLD YOU TO HAND-WASH THOSE CUPS...
I'M SORRY!
SMACK
HE'S GOT NO SPINE...

I'VE SUBTRACTED THE EXTERMINATION FEE FOR THE ROACHES THAT CAME FROM YOUR ROOM.
WHAT?
DETAILS
OH, THAT'S RIGHT!
HEY!!
WHY ARE YOU IN CHARGE OF PAYROLL?
WHAT DO YOU THINK YOU'RE DOING?!
YOU'RE THE ONE WHO'S CONDONING THIS--IT STANDS TO REASON YOU SHOULD BE BILLED FOR GETTING RID OF THEM!
NEVER MIND THAT...
THOSE THINGS BREED ON THEIR OWN!
YOU'VE GOT TO BE JOKING!
AND ANYWAY, HOW DO YOU KNOW THEY'RE FROM MY PLACE?!
WHAT DOES THAT MEAN?!
I CAN TELL JUST BY LOOKING AT THEM.
FLAPPITY
AND YOU TOO, MAKI!
BAP
WHY'S ALL THIS STUFFED IN HERE?
OH...
THIS BULKINESS GOT MY HOPES UP FOR NOTHING.
SORRY... THAT WAS ME.
THE AMOUNT WAS SO PITIFUL, I THOUGHT I'D LEAST MAKE UP FOR IT BY PADDING OUT THE ENVELOPE...
YOU KNOW...
IT'S EVEN MORE DISAPPOINTING.
NIBBLE NIBBLE
MUNCH MUNCH

CRINKLE...
NO MORE UNTIL NEXT SUMMER.
WELL, THIS IS THE LAST OF IT...
I GUESS I WON'T BE EATING ANY MEAT FOR A WHILE, EITHER.
KI
KI KI!
GIMME!
DONATED BY THE NEIGHBORHOOD KIDS.
ZSSH
...
DANGLE
Y- YOU!!
GIVE ME BACK MY EMERGENCY RA--
NO, WAIT.
MY HAMSTER!!

GRAB
PAF
EEP
PLOP
IT'S STILL ALIVE...
WHEW!
EEP EEP!
FEH
POP
WHA... Ш
TWITCH TWITCH
DOCTOOOOOOR-!!!
VWOOOSH

A BATTLE WITH A STRAY CAT OVER YOUR EMERGENCY RATIONS?
HOW UNFORTUNATE.
WELL...DID THE CAT GET THEM?
ISN'T IT A LITTLE EARLY TO TURN TO YOUR EMERGENCY RATIONS ALREADY?
IT WAS ONLY YESTERDAY...
WERE YOU EVEN LISTENING TO MY STORY...?
SO, ANYWAY... I TOOK IT TO THE VET AND WAS GIVEN AN ***OUTRAGEOUS*** MEDICAL BILL.
合計 3,500円
三谷獣医科
TOTAL 3,500 YEN
MITANI VETERINARY CLINIC
AND NOW, I'M IN THE GRIP OF A ***MONSTROUS*** DEBT...
HOW MUCH?
WELL... THAT IS A HUGE FEE FOR TOKU.
BUT HE'S SO TINY! DOESN'T IT SEEM STRANGE HE COSTS SO MUCH TO FIX?!
I MEAN, ***MY*** INJURIES ONLY COST ME 300 YEN...
I THOUGHT IT WOULD BE LIKE 20 YEN!
TO AID YOUR PLIGHT...

IT'S A SECRET?
HE CAME UP FROM OUR SHADOWS?!
GAAAH!
SSSSS
I HAVE INFO ON A SECRET PART-TIME JOB, JUST FOR YOU.
YUP.
IT'S IN THE MEDICAL FIELD, SO IT'S PRETTY PROFIT-ABLE.
MEDICAL? SO THAT MEANS...
OH.
CORPSE-WASHING.
IT'S NOT AS TRICKY AS THAT.
SO THAT MEANS HE'S DONE IT BEFORE...
NO NO
OH, BUT IF IT'S BRAINY WORK, I'M NOT REALLY...
NO PROBLEM, NO PROBLEM.

YOU'LL JUST BE BEEPING THIS BEEP AND BEEPING IT, THAT'S ALL.
IT'S IDEAL, TOKU-- SINCE YOU HAVE SUCH A NICE, HEALTHY BODY...
I'LL PASS...
THAT'S NO PART-TIME JOB!!
OH, THERE YOU ARE.
TOKU.
HERE.
HUH? THIS IS...
I JUST THOUGHT 208 YEN WOULD BE A LITTLE HARD FOR YOU TO LIVE ON.
BOP
I'LL LET YOU PAY OFF THE DAMAGES IN INSTALLMENTS, SO...
...FROM NOW ON, YOU CONCENTRATE ON NOT BREAKING ANY-MORE THINGS, AND...

WOW, BOSS!! THERE'S BROWN-COLORED BILLS IN HERE!
NO WAY!
DID YOU EVEN HEAR ME...?
THANK YOU VERY MUCH!!
NOW I CAN EAT (MEAT, IN PARTICULAR)!
AND PAY BACK MY DEBT!
I SAID, DID YOU HEAR M--
AND BUY SUN-FLOWERS!!
SUN-FLOWERS?
GOOD FOR HIM.
THAT AMOUNT... IT WOULD BE JUST A MERE PITTANCE TO US.
BUT HE'S SO HAPPY...
HEY, IT'S NO FUN TO SEE SOMEONE ATTAIN FULFILLMENT WITHOUT ANY EFFORT, ISN'T IT?
TCH
COME ON, NOW...EVERY ONE GET TO WORK ALREADY.
YES, SIR.

MEAT, MEAT♪
STOP BEING SO GIDDY, AND WATCH YOUR STEP!
MUSH
OKAAAY!
WHOA! SUKE?!
HISS
SORRY ...!
WAIT, IS THAT YOUR MAD FACE?
SLAM
CRASH
BANG
TINKLE
FLAP
FLAP
FLAP
TOKU...

I'M VERY SORR-
ZIP
OH...
YOU TWO WORK NEXT MONTH FOR FREE.
THAT'S THE BEST I CAN DO.
WHAT?!
ME TOO?!
THE BROWN BILLS...
EXCHANGE.
お見舞
SYMPATHY GIFT ¥ 3,500
ALTHOUGH IT'S UNCLEAR WHETHER THE TWO CONSENTED TO THIS AGREEMENT...
...
ACT NOW AND GET AN INTRODUCTION TO A PROFITABLE BLACK MARKET ROUTE!
FORGET IT...
THE EMERGENCY RATIONS STILL LOOK SAFE...FOR NOW.

Tiny の 第8話 Chapter

What if he gets into an accident?!
Calm down.
That's right.
He left his footprints.
Why don't we trace the footprints?
Good idea.
Suke!
Where are you?
BOW BOW

Answer me!
Suke...
Suke--
Su--ke...

How far are we going?
Hey, over there!
Did we find him?!
PATAN..
What's wrong? Where did you guys go?
Uhmm...just around the corner...

第9話 Chapter

SO...
ONE MORE STORE AND WE'RE DONE.
WE'RE ALWAYS SHOPPING, AREN'T WE?
BUT WHY...
WHY IS THERE SO MUCH STUFF TO BUY...?
DON'T ASK ME.
ASK MR. TARO.
READY...
ATTACK...

WHOOSH
MAH JONG SINGLE PLAYERS WELCOME
SMASH
YAH!
WHOA?!
BOOF
?!
WHA ?!
TAAAAHHH!!
BASH
WHOOSH
WHAT'S WITH YOU GU--
...AHH ?!
WHAM
HIYAH!
THWAP
THUD
OW!!

SLAM
BAM
WHAM
YAH!
SNAP
KRAK
BOP
BLAM
OW!
YOU!
BONK
TAKE THAT!
WHAM
ARRRGH!
CUT IT
OUT!!
WHOA!
!!
TOSS
POP
PPP
POP
POP
POP
AAGH!
RETREAT!
CLAK

OH? YOU TOOK IT IN?
YEAH.
SOMEONE SCRIBBLED ON IT AGAIN.
THERE'S BEEN A RASH OF IT RECENTLY.
SQUEAK
I KNOW... I WONDER WHO'S BEHIND IT ALL...
SNEAK
SNEAK
MAKI!!
HI·YAH!
BONK
DON'T THROW THIS AT ME JUST TO CALL ME OVER!!
WHAT ARE YOU DOING?!
COME HERE.

HAVE YOU SEEN WHOEVER'S RESPONSIBLE FOR THI--
WHAT?
TARO, TARO... THIS IS WHERE WE'RE SUPPOSED TO LAUGH.
NO, IT ISN'T!
OH.
RIGHT.
I WAS JUST TAKING A BREAK OUT BACK WHEN SOME BRATS AMBUSHED ME.
THEY LAUNCHED THEIR TOY TOPS AT ME!
JEEZ.
GO!
BAM!

SO ON THAT NOTE, I'LL BE TAKING THE REST OF THE DAY OFF...
STOP DREAMING AND GET TO WORK!
IF I GO OUT ON THE FLOOR WITH THIS HALF-PANDA LOOK, THE GIRLS WILL BE SO WORRIED THAT THEY WON'T BE ABLE TO SLEEP AT NIGHT.
THEN I'LL MAKE IT A MATCHING PAIR FOR YOU! GIVE ME YOUR FACE.
BOP!
OW!
I'M BACK.
OH, HI.
DID SOME-THING HAPPEN?
WELL, MAKI CAME HOME CRYING BECAUSE HE WAS BULLIED BY SOME NEIGHBOR-HOOD KIDS...
NO, I DIDN'T!!
OH, WHAT A COINCI-DENCE.
MR. TOKU WAS JUST ATTACKED BY SOME KIDS, TOO.
THUD

TOKU?!
THEY BOMBARDED HIM WITH FIRECRACKERS.
I SEE JUN ESCAPED UNSCATHED, AS USUAL...
PERHAPS THOSE TWO EMIT SOME KIND OF VIBE THAT KEEPS CHILDREN AWAY?
OR MAYBE THEY REPEATEDLY BUST ONTO SCHOOL GROUNDS AND COMMIT WEIRD BEHAVIOR...
NO, WE DON'T!!
LIKE SHIROW MON-YO
THEN PERHAPS IT'S A TREND...
THE "IDIOT-LOOKING-WAITER HUNT"...
HUNT THREE AND GOOD LUCK WILL COME TO YOU!
THERE'S NO SUCH THING!
OH.
WHAT?
THAT JUST REMINDED ME.
I HAVE A LETTER FOR MR. MAKI.
HUH? ♡
HERE.
DOESN'T IT OCCUR TO YOU TO ASK WHICH PART OF THAT CONVERSATION REMINDED HIM OF YOU?
FOOL...

WAIT... THIS IS FROM THAT JUNIOR CLASS-MATE OF YOURS...
OH. IS THAT STILL GOING ON?
SHE'S VERY PER-SISTENT.
IT'S NOT "GOING ON"!
IT'S ALL ONE-SIDED, FROM HER!
DON'T BE EMBAR-RASSED.
IF YOU DON'T WRITE BACK, SHE'LL HURT YOU.
UGH...
I'M NOT SAYING A WORD...
HA! は
OH, ARE YOU AWAKE?
WHAT AM I DOING ON THE FLOOR?
HUH?
WHY THE NEWS-PAPERS?
BECAUSE TARO SAID NOT TO LAY "THAT THING" ON THE WORK COUNTER.
?
SORRY TO ASK YOU SO SOON AFTER RECOVERY, BUT COULD YOU TAKE OUT THE TRASH?
OH, OKAY.

OOF.
IT WON'T FIT...
SQUISH

HUH?!
REALLY?!
CLAK
MR. TOKU, WHILE YOU'RE AT IT, CAN YOU WASH OUT THE TRASH CAN...
HUH?
HE'S GONE...?

TOKU'S GONE?
ISN'T HE ON THE LATE SHIFT TODAY?
I WONDER IF HE WENT HOME...
HE WOULDN'T LEAVE WITHOUT EATING THE LEFT-OVERS.
THEN HE'S...
...ABDUCT-ED.
LID
TOKU'S COMPLETELY WORTH-LESS.
DON'T MAKE HOLES EVERY-WHERE!
AND ANYWAY, WHO WOULD PAY THE RANSOM...?
HIS HAMSTERS, MAYBE?
SECRET SAVINGS!

10 YEN?! 10 YEN!!
WHAT A KING'S RANSOM.
WELL, I'M SURE HE'LL BE BACK SOON.
UNTIL THEN...MAKI, TAKE HIS SHIFT.
WHA?
NO WAY...
AND HE STILL AIN'T BACK!
LAST TRASH OF THE DAY.
BLAM
DAMN! TODAY'S JUST NOT MY DAY...
TOKU!!
U...
UM...

MR. MA...
BONK
SHUT UP! FLAKING OUT LIKE THAT!
WHAT'S GOING ON?!
BECAUSE OF YOU, I HAD TO TAKE UP THE SLACK!
I HAD TO WASH OUT THE TRASH CANS IN THIS COLD! MY SCHEDULE WAS COMPLETELY SCREWED UP! AND I WAS FORCED TO RECEIVE A LETTER I DIDN'T WANT!
WHAT ARE YOU GONNA DO ABOUT IT?!
I HAD MY OWN PROBLEMS!
IN MY OWN WAY...
WHAT ARE YOU TALK--
DAH!
WONK
WHOA!
LEAVE MY UNDERLING ALONE.
JAK

SO, TOKU.
THIS IS THE GUY?
YES, THAT'S RIGHT.
WHAT THE HECK?
ARE YOU SERIOUS?
THIS? NO WAY!
YOU'RE NOT JUST MAKING IT UP, ARE YOU?
NO, NEVER!
?
OH!
YOU'RE THE BRATS FROM EARLIER! WITH THE TOPS!!
THEY'RE CALLED BEY-BLADES, OLD MAN.
WHO ARE YOU CALLING AN OLD MAN?!
YOU, OLD MAN.
AND YOU! WHY ARE YOU BEING SO WEAK WITH THESE BRATS?!
UH... WELL, THERE'S A REASON FOR THIS...
WHAT'S WITH THE "UNDERLING" CRAP?!
GRAB
?!

OKAY, LET'S GO.
GO WHERE...
I MEAN, LEMME GO!!
PLEASE... JUST THINK OF IT AS HELPING ME SAVE FACE, AND COME ALONG QUIETLY.
WHAT THE HELL IS THAT?!
NO WAY!
I'M SORRY, MR. MAKI.
JUST LET ME GO!
SLIP
HUH?
WHAM!
MR. MAKI?!
ARE YOU SURE HE'S THE ONE?
I'M BEGINNING TO HAVE MY DOUBTS, TOO...

...
...
UH...
OH.
HE'S UP.
HUH?

YOU BRATS!
CLATTER
GKRAK
OW OW OW OW OW!!
LOSER!
DON'T WRECK THE PLACE. IT'S A REAL DUMP.
WHAT DO I CARE?!
WOBBLE WOBBLE
CREAK
IF YOU DON'T WANT ME TO WRECK IT, *UNTIE* MY HANDS!!
STOMP
STOMP
STOMP
STOMP
HOW IMMA-TURE.
WHOA!
WELL...
WE DON'T CARE EITHER...
BUT YOU'LL MAKE THE OWNER CRY.
PLEASE DON'T DESTROY MY HOME...
......
BY THE WAY... DON'T YOU HAVE ANY FOOD IN THIS HOUSE?

UMM... I'VE ONLY GOT SOME TEA...
SERIOUS-LY? LAME!
AT LEAST HAVE SOME JUICE ON-HAND! YOU'RE AN ADULT, AREN'T YOU?
BUT THESE TEA LEAVES ARE SUPPOSED TO BE PRETTY GOOD.
I SEE...
HEY, TOKU.
WAIT! IT'S PAST THE EXPIRATION DATE!
WELL, YEAH...THE STORE WAS GOING TO THROW IT OUT, BUT THEY SAID I COULD HAVE IT.
HEY.
DON'T SERVE US SOME-THING LIKE THAT!!
THEN GO OUT AND GET US SOMETHING, WILL YOU? WE'LL GIVE YOU MONEY.
HEY...
LIS-TEN...
KRASH
WHAT ARE YOU BLENDING IN FOR? WITH THESE BRATS!
YOU TRAI-TOR!!
EVEN LENDING THEM YOUR ROOM!
WHAT?
WATCH IT!
BUT MR. MAKI...YOU SELF-DESTRUCT ED, SO I BROUGHT YOU HERE. I DIDN'T WANT YOU TO CATCH COLD.
TH--
THAT WAS BE-CAUSE YOU...
MUMBLE MUMBLE
BUT YOU'RE AT THESE BRATS' COMMAND JUST BECAUSE OF THAT?
WHAT, DID THEY FEED YOU OR SOME-THING?!
HOW DID YOU KNOW?
THEY GAVE ME A MEAT BUN.
THEY BEAT ME UP AFTER THAT, THOUGH.

THEY EVEN GAVE ME A CABBAGE!
¥250-
じどん
AND A WHOLE ONE, AT THAT!
つとね
TA-DAH
LEADER, YOU'RE SO GENEROUS!
HOW NICE FOR YOU...
SO, OLD MAN.
I SAID, WHO ARE YOU CALLING AN OLD MAN?!
THERE'S SOMETHING I WANT TO DISCUSS WITH YOU.
WHAT?
I DON'T HAVE ANYTHING TO SAY TO Y--
WHAM
CHAK
MAKI LOVES DISCUSSIONS. ♡
SZZZ
TEE HEE!
GOOD.
HOW HUMIL-IATING...

AT YOUR STORE...
THERE'S A GIRL NAMED "AIRI" THAT COMES IN AS A CUSTOMER, RIGHT?
AIRI? WAS THERE SOMEONE WITH THAT NAME?
HUH?!
WHAT'S THAT?
JUST BREAK UP WITH HER!
BREAK UP WITH HER.
BUT I'M NOT SEEING HER...
...OR RATHER, I DON'T EVEN KNOW WHO SHE IS!
I HEARD THAT YOU INSTINCTIVELY GO AFTER ALL THE WOMEN CUSTOMERS!
IF THAT'S TRUE, YOU MUST KNOW WHO SHE IS!
I CHAT 'EM UP, BUT THAT'S ALL!
AND WHO DID YOU HEAR THAT FROM, ANYWAY?!
LOOK, A CABBAGE!

ARE YOU SURE HE'S THE ONE?
WHAT ARE YOU TALKING ABOUT?
HEY...
NOW I KNOW JUST EXACTLY WHAT YOU THINK OF ME!
OW OW! I COULDN'T HELP IT!
I WAS SUDDENLY CAPTURED AND HAD A HARD TIME, TOO!
YOU WERE JUST PLAYING WITH THEM!
OWW!
OW OW OW!
BUT, YOU'RE THE ONLY LOGICAL ONE TO BLAME WHEN THERE'S A WOMAN INVOLVED...!
TOKU!!!
TAKE THIS!
THUMP THUMP THUMP
ANYONE WITH COMMON SENSE WOULD GIVE HIM THE COLD SHOULDER.
YOU DID NOT!
I CALLED!
WELL...
YOU DID NOT!
IT'S JUST THAT I CAN'T BELIEVE SHE'D GO OUT WITH A DORK LIKE HIM.
HOW WAS I SUPPOSED TO KNOW WHAT WAS HAPPENING TO YOU?!
I PHONED, DIDN'T I?
YEAH... I DID.
STOP CALLING ME "LEADER."
LEADER, YOU PUT IN A THREATENING CALL TO THE STORE, RIGHT?!
...TELLING THEM YOU ABDUCTED ME?!
HUH?!
I DON'T WANT TO BELIEVE IT EITHER, BUT...
WHOA!
LEADER!!
GRAB

BUT NOBODY CAME FOR YOU, SO WE HAD TO COME DOWN OURSELVES.
HMM...
MAN, YOU SURE ARE TAKEN FOR GRANTED.
DOOOOM
I SEE... SO THAT'S WHY...
SNIFF
I TOLD YOU, I DON'T KNOW ABOUT ANY SUCH PHONE CALL...
KNOWING, AND YET IGNORING...
INDEED, THIS WORLD IS FULL OF MYSTERY...
DUN DUN
SH-THUNK
!!
HUH?!
HOW EASILY THESE DOORS SLIDE OPEN IN SUCH A DAMP ENVIRONMENT...
HOW DID YOU GET IN THERE ...?
WHO'S THIS?!
A FRIEND?
UH... NO...
YOU GUYS...
WHAT A SNEAKILY CRUEL THING TO SAY...

TO SOMEONE LIKE ME WHO TOOK THE THREATENING PHONE CALL, THEN LEFT THE STORE OUT OF SHEER WORRY FOR YOU...
SST...
...THAT'S NOT A VERY NICE THING TO SAY, IS IT?
I KNEW IT... SO HE'S THE ONE AT THE CENTER OF THIS STORM OF BAD LUCK...
YOU SHOW UP PRETTY LATE FOR SOMEONE SO WORRIED.
I WAS SCOPING THE PLACE FOR AN ENTRY ROUTE.
IT'S OKAY... I'M JUST HAPPY YOU CAME.
EVEN NOW THAT YOU'RE MY ENEMY...
NO, YOU SEE...
DRIBBLE
I JUST COULDN'T FORGIVE THE FACT THAT YOU GUYS WERE IN DANGER SOMEWHERE... WHERE I WASN'T THERE TO SEE.
TURN
NOW, THEN.
OKAY, CHILDREN.
SST...
PLAYTIME IS OVER.

CLATTER
CLATTER
THUD
IF YOU'RE GOING TO DO SOMETHING RIGHT, YOU HAVE TO GIVE IT YOUR ALL.
YOU DIDN'T COME HERE TO RESCUE US?!
SHOW NO MERCY!!
MAKI... ON THE ROAD TO TRUE MANHOOD, ONE MUST OVERCOME MANY DANGERS...
JUST LEAVE ALREADY!
A CELL PHONE?
WHOA! THE PHONE LIST IS FULL OF WOMEN'S NAMES!
WHAT THE HECK IS THIS?
AND LOOK AT HOW MANY THERE ARE!
672 LISTINGS?!
WHA ...?

OH, THIS IS MR. MAKI'S PHONE.
WHAT ...!
HMM...IT MUST'VE FALLEN OUT WITH THOSE OTHER THINGS JUST NOW.
MINA-GAWA... WHAT ARE YOU DOING WITH MY PHONE...?
!!
MISS AIRI'S NUMBER MAY BE IN THERE!
OH, RIGHT!
HEY! DON'T TOUCH SOMEONE ELSE'S PROPERTY ...!
DANG, IT'S PASSWORD PRO-TECTED.
HMM...
WHEW
MAKI'S BIRTH-DAY IS MARCH THIRD.
TRY IT!
MINA ...!!
0303...
POP
OOH, IT WORKED.
IT'S QUICKER IF YOU USE 'SEARCH'.
SEARCH?
PUSH 'MENU' - THEN PUSH THE ● BUTTON, TOGETHER WITH...
ぱっ
BLIP
全件データ削除しました
ALL DATA HAS BEEN DELETED
OH...
WHY?
HUH? WHAT'S WRONG?
HEY.

みし…
CREAK…
WHA?!
SMASH
STOMP
!!
SHFFT

AAAAGGGHHHH
WHOA!
STOP!
EEK!
U-UHH...
WHAM
OH? MR. MAKI.
CRUNCH
FANCY MEETING YOU HERE.
HUH?! JUN?!
I GOT A CALL FROM MR. MINA-GAWA, AND--
NEVER MIND THE SMALL TALK! STOP THEM!
THEM?
MISS MAKI-SHIMA.
ISN'T THAT ENOUGH?
STOP

S...
URGH!!
BUMP
OH... WE'VE MET BEFORE.
GOOD WORK!
YES.
WHUMP
SIR! MY UNWORTHY YOUNG BROTHER HAS CAUSED YOU MUCH TROUBLE!
I APOLOGIZE MOST SINCERELY!
THUD!!
NOW, NOW... PLEASE RAISE YOUR HEAD.
SIBLINGS...?
YES. IT'S BEEN ON MY MIND EVER SINCE MR. TOKU WAS ATTACKED...
THEY LOOK SO ALIKE.
I'M GLAD I BROUGHT HER ALONG.
OH... I SEE.
WHY SHOULD YOU HAVE TO APOLOGIZE, BIG SISTER?!

YOU'RE TOO GOOD-NATURED TO SEE THAT HE'S *FOOLING* YOU!
HURRY AND JUST BREAK UP WITH HIM ALREADY!
HEY...
WAIT A SECOND...
THIS... THIS IS "AIRI"?!
AIRI MAKISHIMA 16 YEARS OLD ❤
SO YOU *DID* KNOW HER AFTER ALL.
WELL, YES-- AND NO... IT'S JUST... SOMETHING I'D LIKE TO FORGET...
DON'T ASK...
I SAW YOU!
I'VE SEEN MY SISTER MEETING YOU BE-HIND THAT STORE...
OW!
NOOGIE
NOOGIE
NOOGIE
ENOUGH.
OW OWW! I'M SORRY, SISTER...!
UME-BOSHI...
OH!
YOU MUST HAVE MISTAKEN HIM FOR ME.
I'VE HAD MISS MAKISHIMA COME DOWN TO THE STORE SEVERAL TIMES WHEN I HAD SOME ORDERS TO HAND DOWN TO HER.
WHO ARE YOU?
HE'S MR. ICHINO-MIYA, THE SEMPAI WHOM I SERVE!
GOOD EVENING!

SERVE?! THIS GIRLY-LOOKING ...?!
DAAAH!!
SHUT UP!
NO, LEADER! YOU MUSTN'T!!
NO, NO... HE'S JUST A CHILD. I WON'T GET MAD.
HUH?
REALLY?
IT SEEMS LIKE THIS WAS ALL BECAUSE HE WAS WORRIED ABOUT HIS SISTER...
SO LET'S FORGIVE HIM THIS TIME.
EASY FOR YOU TO SAY, SINCE YOU WERE COMPLETELY UNHARMED...
BUT...
CREAK...
...THERE WON'T BE A NEXT TIME.
LET'S STOP RIGHT THERE...
AH, ALL'S WELL THAT ENDS WELL...
IT'S NOT WELL!!
MY-MY MEMORIES OF LOVE--
THEY'VE GONE 'POOF'!

THINK OF IT THIS WAY... NOW YOU'LL HAVE THE JOY OF COMPLETING YOUR LIST ANEW.
I DON'T WANT TO HEAR IT FROM THE VERY CROOK WHO WAS RESPON-SIBLE!!
LOOK ON THE BRIGHT SIDE!
OH, THEN...
CLUNK
...I'LL HAVE THE CELL PHONE NUMBERS OF ALL MY JUNIOR CLASSMATES ENTERED INTO YOUR PHONE.
I'LL TELL THE GIRL WHO SENT YOU THE LETTER TO SEND E-MAIL TO YOU AT THIS NUMBER FROM NOW ON, TOO.
SO! I LEAVE IT TO YOU.
YES.
NOOOOOOO!!!
DOWN, BOY.
AND SO, THE CURTAINS CLOSE ON THIS LITTLE INCIDENT...
TADADADADA
TATATATA
...LEAVING MAKI'S CELL PHONE CHOCK FULL OF E-MAIL...
...A PHOTO ATTACHMENT...
SHUT THAT THING UP.

Tiny の
第9話
Chapter
The year's already over.
A year passes by so quickly.
We have to make preparations for the New Year.
Right.
To prepare for New Year's, we need...

Kurikinton (mashed sweet potatoes with whole chestnuts), Onishime (stewed vegetables), Kazunoko (herring roe), Kamaboko (fishcake)...
And datemaki (sweet rolled egg), too.
Well, let's start making it.
Okaaay!
And...
Shimeka-zari!
...Kagami-mochi.
...The New Year festive foods.
I've finished cutting the veggies.
Putting some old nails in the pot will keep the beans shiny.
We can't forget the ham.
Yeah.

Done!!
Kurikinton...
Let's call the boss and have a taste!
OK.
Wake up.
GAN
Wow, you guys made this?

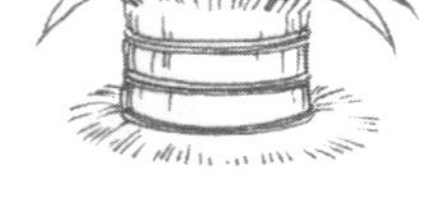

CONTINUED IN VOLUME 3

Café 吉祥寺で

HELLO. WORN OUT IN BOTH BODY AND SOUL, THIS IS NEGISHI.

I'VE SUNK SO LOW THAT I CAN NOW ONLY FIT IN THE "S" SIZE PANTS OF MY DREAMS UP TO MY KNEES...
IF I CAN'T GET IN SHAPE ENOUGH TO WEAR THEM BY THIS SUMMER, THEY ARE FATED TO BE STOLEN AWAY BY MY LITTLE SISTER--
THOSE "S" SIZE PANTS.

BUT ENOUGH ABOUT ALL OF THAT.

SO. VOLUME TWO. IT'S OUT.
I'M SHOCKED. IT'S TRULY AMAZING THAT PUBLICATION CONTINUES, EVEN WHEN THE ADMIRABLE STATEMENTS IN MY AFTERWORD OF THE PREVIOUS VOLUME SHOW NO SIGN AT ALL OF COMING TRUE. STILL CONTINUE TO STRUGGLE, TAXED TO THE LIMIT. YES, IT'S IMPORTANT TO KNOW YOUR LIMITATIONS, BUT WHY MUST I FIND THEM OUT NOW, DEAR GOD? THIS IS ABOUT THE 53RD TIME I'VE ENCOUNTERED MY LIMITS... IF I HAD OVERCOME THEM EACH TIME BEFORE, COULD I HAVE BEEN A SUPER SAIYAN (LEVEL ONE) BY NOW? FRIEZAAAA!!!!!!!
(NOW IN INCOHERENT MODE)...
OH WELL. (HUH?)
THIS AUTHOR IS FULL OF SUCH PITIFUL THOUGHTS, BUT I WILL BE HAPPY IF YOU SAY, "WHO CARES!" AND JUST HAVE FUN ENJOYING--
OR RIDICULING--THIS VOLUME.

UNTIL NEXT TIME!

KYOKO NEGISHI

ALMOST CRYING
by Mako Takahashi
Please adopt me...
Abandoned in a park as a child, Aoi finds a new home with Gaku.
Growing up brings new emotions, new love, and new jealousies.
DMP
DIGITAL MANGA PUBLISHING
ISBN# 1-56970-909-2 $12.95
yaoi-manga.com
The girls only sanctuary
© 2002 Mako Takahashi. All rights reserved. First published in Japan in 2002by HOUBUNSHA CO.LTD., Tokyo.
English translation rights in United States and Canada arranged with HOUBUNSHA CO., LTD. through Tuttle-Mori Agency, Inc. Tokyo.

YOU & HARUJION
by Keiko Kinoshita
All is lost . . .
Haru has just lost his father, Yakuza-esque creditors are coming to collect on his father's debts, and the bank has foreclosed the mortgage on the house…
When things go from bad to worse, in steps Yuuji Senoh…
ISBN# 1-56970-925-4 $12.95
DMP
DIGITAL MANGA PUBLISHING
yaoi-manga.com
The girls only sanctuary
© Keiko Kinoshita 2004. Originally published in Japan in 2004 by Taiyo Tosho Co., Ltd.

LOST BOYS
"Will you be our father?"
by Kaname Itsuki
A boy named "Air" appears at Mizuki's window one night and transports him to Neverland.
ISBN# 1-56970-924-6 $12.95
© Kaname Itsuki 2004. Originally published in Japan in 2004 by Taiyo Tosho Co., Ltd.
DMP
DIGITAL MANGA PUBLISHING
yaoi-manga.com
The girls only sanctuary

DMP
Beyond My Touch
When a little thing like **death** gets in the way of love. A special ghost's affections, will come back from the **beyond.**
yaoi-manga.com
The girls only sanctuary
ISBN# 1-56970-928-9 $12.95
Beyond My Touch - Meniwa Sayakani Mienedomo © TOMO MAEDA 2003.
Originally published in Japan in 2003 by SHINSHOKAN Co., LTD

OUR KINGDOM
When the Prince falls for the Pauper...
The family inheritance will be the last of their concerns.
Written & Illustrated by
Naduki Koujima
Volume 1 ISBN# 1-56970-935-1 $12.95
Volume 2 ISBN# 1-56970-914-9 $12.95
Volume 3 ISBN# 1-56970-913-0 $12.95
Volume 4 ISBN# 1-56970-912-2 $12.95
DMP
DIGITAL MANGA PUBLISHING
yaoi-manga.com
The girls only sanctuary
Our Kingdom © 2000 Naduki Koujima

DMP
La Esperança
yaoi-manga.com
The girls only sanctuary
Despite young Georges popularity, he has never been able to truly forge a close bond with others. That is, of course, until he met Robert!
But after time, will Georges come to regret it?
Mystery surrounds him and only a tragic clue from the past may provide the answer.
La Esperança
1
Yaoi Manga
VOL. 1 ISBN# 1-56970-933-5 $12.95
VOL. 2 ISBN# 1-56970-932-7 $12.95
VOL. 3 ISBN# 1-56970-931-9 $12.95
VOL. 4 ISBN# 1-56970-930-0 $12.95
VOL. 5 ISBN# 1-56970-929-7 $12.95

Digital Manga has the best in Boy's Love!
Identical Rings, Strange Love...
ONLY THE RING FINGER KNOWS
ONLY THE RING FINGER KNOWS
その指だけが知っている
By
Satoru Kannagi
Hotaru Odagiri
DMP
YAOI SERIES
By
Satoru Kannagi
Hotaru Odagiri
ISBN# 1-56970-980-7
Price $12.95
Go to our website and see what other great Yaoi titles we have!
www.dmpbooks.com
AVAILABLE NOW!

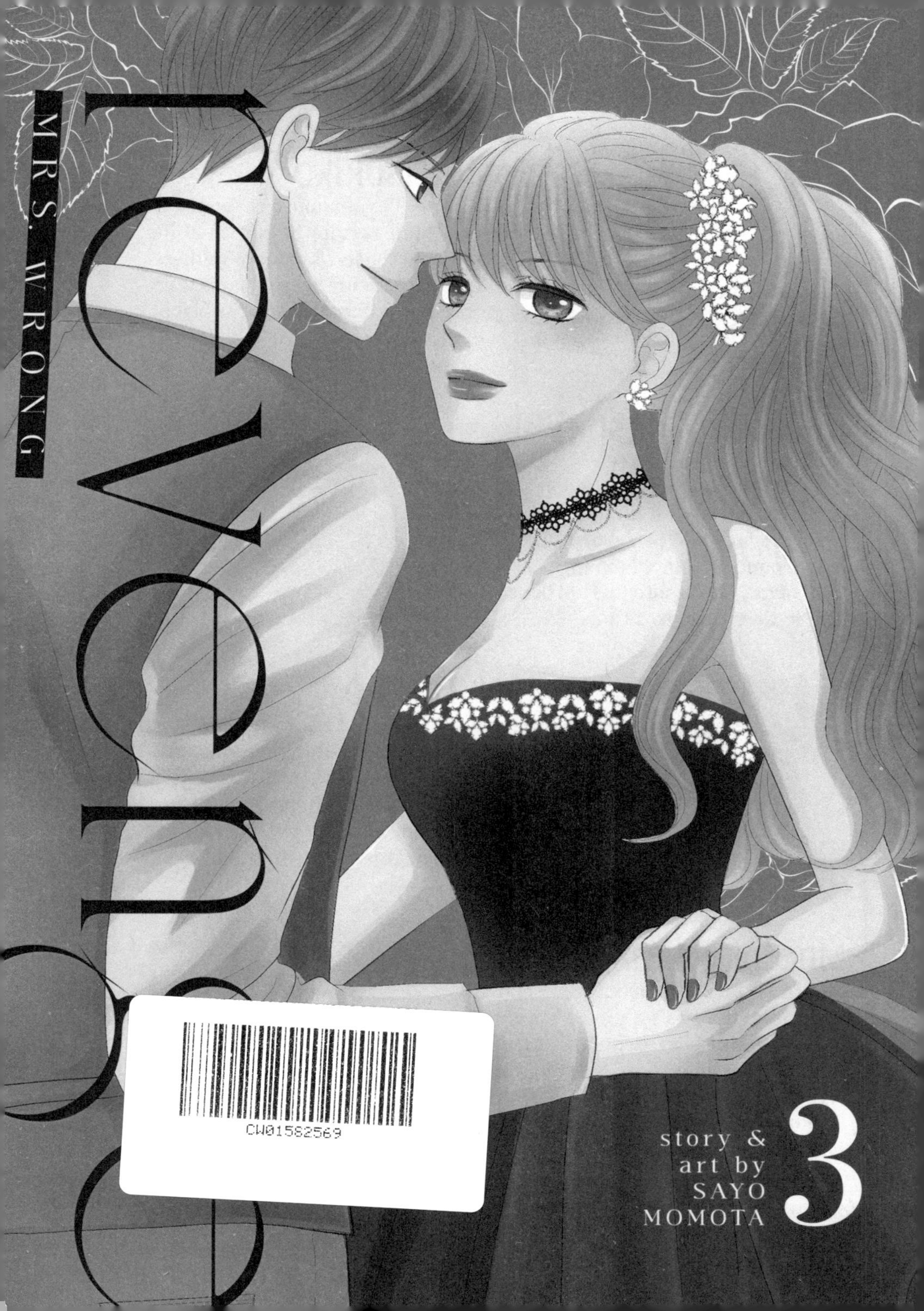
revenge
MRS. WRONG
story & art by SAYO MOMOTA
3

CHARACTERS

Kamishiro Tsukiko

Raised alongside her glamorous younger sister, Mitsuki. While serving as her stand-in, she fell hard for her sister's fiancé. Tsukiko attempted to steal him for herself...and then became pregnant. Currently works from home.

Kamishiro Mitsuki

Tsukiko's younger sister. Always puts herself first. While dealing with what she believes is HSDD, she slept with several guys despite being engaged. When word of her cheating got around at her company, her coworker (and lover) Muramoto invited her to live with him in New York for a time.

Yoshioka Akito

An attractive employee of a trading company and Mitsuki's fiancé. He hates girls who only judge guys by how they look on paper. When he discovered that he and Mitsuki have some commonalities, they got engaged. Now aware of Tsukiko's deception, he finds himself afraid of her...

Muramoto Takeashi

Mitsuki's former friend with benefits and colleague. He was on top of his game at the company and very popular with the ladies, but his feelings for Mitsuki were real. Unaware that Tsukiko was standing in for Mitsuki, he raped her. After that, he began to help Tsukiko with her plan...

◆ Plain Tsukiko and glamorous Mitsuki are identical twins. Mitsuki takes advantage of their uneven relationship and sometimes makes Tsukiko stand in for her on her myriad dates.

◆ One day, Tsukiko stood in for Mitsuki at a marriage planning session with Mitsuki's fiancé. They ended up back at Akito's place, where he made passionate love to Tsukiko. When he told her she was behaving differently, Tsukiko took that as him truly seeing her and fell genuinely in love with him.

◆ Tsukiko believed she could make Akito happier than her promiscuous sister...and so she walked down the aisle with him. Mitsuki was worried by her sister's unusual behavior. When Tsukiko's pregnancy was revealed, the battle between the twins reached new heights...or perhaps new lows...

STORY

revenge

MRS. WRONG

contents

revenge

MRS. WRONG

Chapter 11

ガタッ
KLATTA
AH!
MN!
HUFF!
MN...

SQUEEZE
...!
AH!
HNF!
HAAH!
TO THE BED. NOW.

FWMP

MY HEART WON'T STOP POUNDING.
IT'S LIKE THE FIRST TIME ALL OVER AGAIN.
I FEEL IT TOO.
MM...!
AH...!
CREAK

FWP
BA-THMP
YOU'RE LIKE A TOTALLY DIFFERENT PERSON.
YEAH?

YOU ARE TOO.
CREAK...
PINCH
JOLT
MM...!
LICK

びくん
QUIVER
KISS
NO...!
I'M SORRY!
WAS THAT NOT GOOD?
NO, IT'S JUST...

IT FELT TOO GOOD. IT SURPRISED ME...
MITSUKI...!
PLEASE...
KEEP GOING...

UNTIL NOW...
AH...
NO MATTER HOW ANYONE TOUCHED ME, I WOULDN'T FEEL A THING...
HF!
AH!
NN...!
AM I LIVING IN THE SAME BODY?
SHLP...
...!
YOU'RE GETTING SOAKED.

HUH?
NO WAY...
YEAH...
SEE? RIGHT THROUGH THESE PANTIES.
AH...!
I CAN'T...!
AKITO-SAN...!
SHLK

AH...!
TREMBLE
...!
HAAH...
I...
CAN...

FEEL SOME-THING NOW?
IT'S AMAZING...

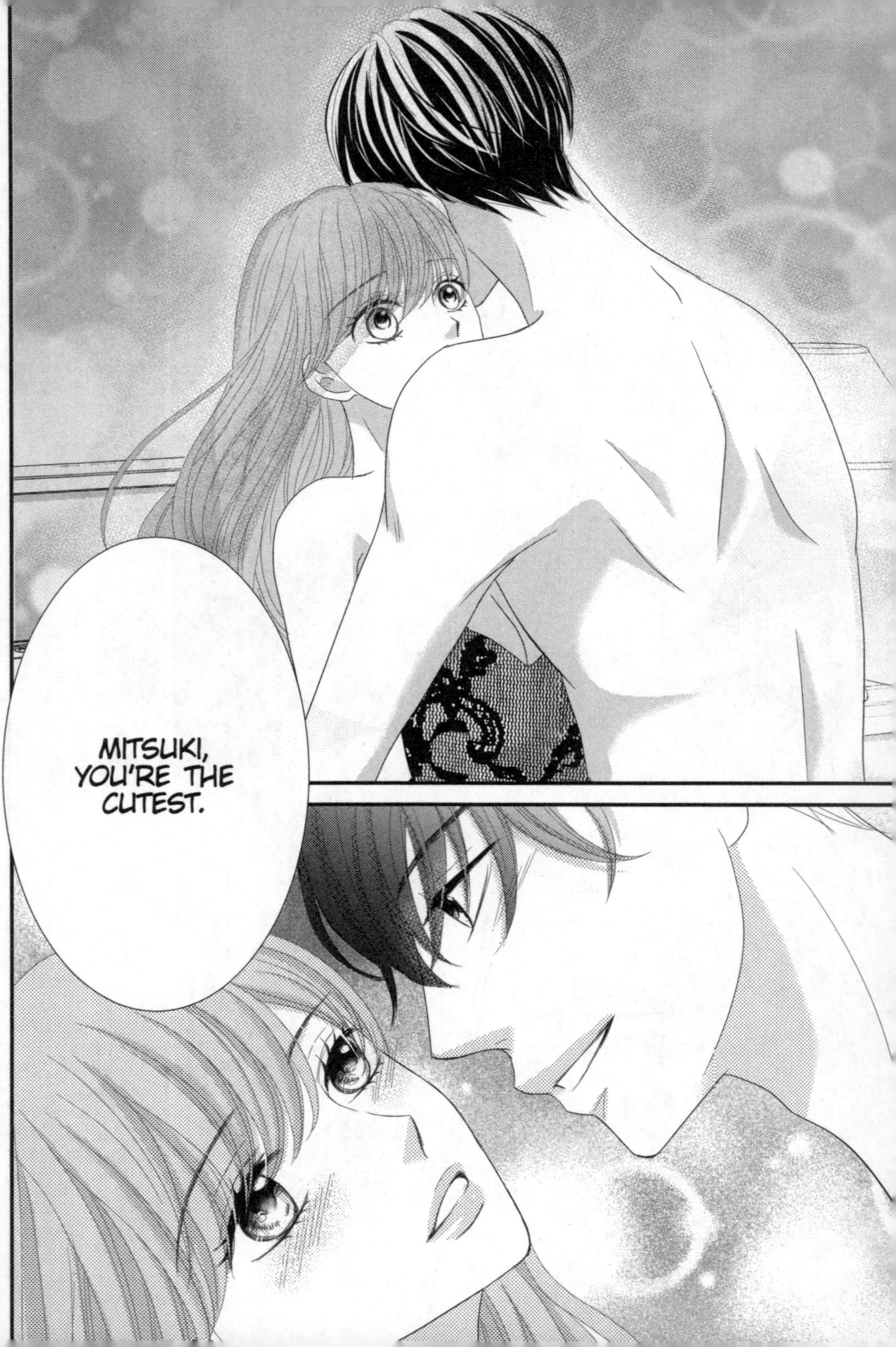
MITSUKI, YOU'RE THE CUTEST.

CREAK...
...
!

...!
AKITO-SA--
MITSUKI...
I LOVE YOU.

THIS MITSUKI, HERE IN MY ARMS... YOU'RE THE ONE I LOVE.

AKITO-SAN.
WHENEVER I HAD SEX, I ALWAYS FELT...
AN ABSENCE WHERE THERE SHOULD HAVE BEEN FIRE.
AH...!

WHAT IS THIS?
EVERY-WHERE AKITO TOUCHES ME...
I MELT.
YOU SEE?
YOU'RE STARTING TO OVER-FLOW.
...!

CAN SEX...
REALLY BE SO DIFFER-ENT?
AH...!
GNG
YOU ALMOST THERE?

I'M JUST ABOUT THERE TOO.
TUG
!
FWMP
LOOK AT ME.

I WANT YOU TO LOOK AT ME.
どきん
BA-THMP

CREAK
CREAK
CREAK
HFF!
AH!
AH!
I...!
I LOVE YOU TOO!
AKITO-SAN!

AH—

IT'S ALREADY NIGHT.
HM?
THINGS ARE COMPLICATED, MITSUKI...
BUT THROUGH ALL THIS MESS, I CAN SEE THAT I REALLY LOVE YOU.

I WANT TO SPEND THE REST OF MY LIFE WITH YOU.
AKITO...
I FEEL THE SAME.

BUT...
WE'LL DEAL WITH YOUR SISTER.
IF WE TAKE OUR TIME AND TALK THINGS OUT, SHE'LL UNDERSTAND. SHE HAS TO.
RIGHT...
I WONDER...
IF TSUKIKO REALLY WILL...

ALL RIGHT, I'M HEADING BACK TO THE APARTMENT FOR A BIT.
IF ANYTHING HAPPENS, CALL ME RIGHT AWAY.
GOT IT.
......

パタ…
PTNK...

ガチャ
KA-CHAK
OH!
WELCOME HOME, DEAR.

Chapter 12

WELCOME HOME, DEAR.

WHAT ARE YOU DOING HERE?
DID YOU GET DIS-CHARGED?
THE IV DRIP HELPED ME FEEL BETTER, SO I ASKED THE DOCTOR TO LET ME GO HOME.
THE BABY IS HEALTHY TOO. I'M SO HAPPY.
OH! AND REMEMBER, WE'RE TURNING IN OUR MARRIAGE REGISTRATION TOMORROW.

OUR MARRIAGE IS VOID.
YOU DO KNOW THAT... DON'T YOU?
WHY IS THAT?
"WHY IS"--?
BECAUSE YOU AREN'T MITSUKI!

HONESTLY? I FIGURED IT OUT SOME TIME AGO.
I HAD NO IDEA WHAT TO DO, SO I JUST PLAYED ALONG UNTIL THE WEDDING.
BUT I CAN'T DO THIS ANYMORE!
THAT'S WONDERFUL.
CLING...

YOU KNEW I WASN'T MITSUKI ALL ALONG. THAT'S WHY YOU WENT THROUGH WITH THE WEDDING, ISN'T IT?
THAT'S PROOF ENOUGH THAT YOU LOVE ME. THAT YOU LOVE OUR BABY.
NO!
I JUST COULDN'T DEAL WITH THE TRUTH. I WAS BEING A COWARD!
CLENCH
BESIDES...

THAT BABY INSIDE YOU ISN'T MINE.
WELL, YES, THERE'S THAT PREMARITAL CHECKUP. BUT THAT'S NOT A HUNDRED PERCENT GUARANTEE YOU CAN'T *EVER* CONCEIVE, IS IT?
THIS BABY IS DEFINITELY YOURS.
JUST THINK OF ALL OUR LOVEMAKING, DAY IN AND DAY OUT...

NO. THE ODDS ARE ASTRO-NOMICALLY LOW.
YOU'RE WONDERING TOO, AREN'T YOU?
IF IT MIGHT BE ANOTHER MAN'S?
......

HOW AWFUL. WHY WOULD YOU SAY SOME-THING LIKE THAT?
WHEN I WAS RAPED BY MURA-MOTO...
I TOLD HIM I WASN'T MITSUKI. OVER AND OVER...
BUT HE WOULDN'T STOP.
AFTER IT HAPPENED, I WANTED TO DIE.
I COULDN'T TELL ANYONE. I SUFFERED ALL ALONE.

......
CLENCH...
BUT...
I BELIEVED I WOULD GET MARRIED TO YOU. I'D LIVE HAPPILY EVER AFTER...
AND BEAR THIS CHILD. **YOUR** CHILD.
WHENEVER I FELL, THAT BELIEF HELPED ME PICK MYSELF UP.

I'M NOT LIKE MITSUKI.
I LOVE ONLY YOU, AKITO-SAN.
SHF...
JUST YOU...
FOREVER AND EVER...

I'M SORRY FOR STAYING WITH YOU, EVEN WHEN I KNEW THE TRUTH.
AND WHAT HAPPENED WITH MURAMOTO IS A NIGHTMARE.
BABY GOODS
I WILL DO WHATEVER I CAN TO MAKE UP FOR IT.
BUT PLEASE, YOU HAVE TO UNDERSTAND...
I CAN'T MARRY YOU.

......
SHE FINALLY UNDER-STANDS...
DOESN'T SHE?
HEE HEE...

SHF...
IT'S OKAY.
YOU'RE JUST CONFUSED RIGHT NOW, AKITO-SAN.
AFTER ALL, YOU LOVE ME.
HEY...
DO YOU REMEMBER WHEN I WAS STANDING IN FOR **HER**, ON OUR FIRST DATE?

YOU'RE COMPLETELY DIFFERENT.
YOU'RE THE ONLY ONE WHO EVER SAW IT WAS ME.
IT MADE ME SO HAPPY.
THE FACT THAT I CAN BE MYSELF WITH YOU NOW MAKES ME SO HAPPY.
YOU'RE MY SOULMATE.
I LOVE YOU...
AKITO-SAN.

SHE ISN'T LISTENING.
I'M NOT GETTING THROUGH TO HER AT ALL--
KA-CHAK
!
BTNK

NOK NOK
コンコン
ガチャ
KA-CHAK
SQUEEZE...
AKITO-SAN?
WHAT'S WRONG?

...!
HUFF...
MITSUKI...

CREAK
AH...!

EVERY-THING WILL BE ALL RIGHT.
AKITO-SAN WILL COME BACK TO ME.
NO MATTER WHAT.

GOOD MORNING.
MORNING.
I'M MOSTLY OUT OF THE OFFICE TODAY, SO I'LL PROBABLY GET HOME EARLY.
THAT'S GOOD.
AKITO AND I ARE RENTING AN APARTMENT BY THE WEEK, AND THE FIRST WEEK HAS PASSED.
TSUKIKO IS AT THE OLD APARTMENT, SO WE CAN'T GO BACK...
BUT WE'VE MANAGED TO GATHER THE NECESSITIES. SOMEHOW, THINGS HAVE CALMED DOWN.

I CALLED MURAMOTO YESTERDAY. TOLD HIM EVERYTHING THAT WAS GOING ON.
HE WAS PRETTY SHAKEN UP.
WELL... NATURALLY.
TSUKIKO HASN'T REACHED OUT TO YOU?
NO.
BUT SHE WAS SO HUNG UP ON AKITO.
I CAN'T IMAGINE SHE'D JUST LET HIM GO.

MITSUKI.
IT'S ALL RIGHT.
WHATEVER HAPPENS, I'LL PROTECT YOU.
FOR NOW...
I WANT TO KEEP LIVING THIS LIFE TOGETHER WITHOUT WORRY. JUST A LITTLE LONGER...

IT LOOKS LIKE HE'S STILL GOING TO WORK...
BUT HE NEVER COMES HOME.
WHY?
WHERE IS HE NOW?
!
AKITO-SAN!
SHF...
ス

THIS IS...

ドクン
BA-THMP
PTNK...
パタン
WHY IS MITSUKI THERE?!

THOSE TWO...
DID THEY MAKE UP?!
THWAK
IMPOS-SIBLE.
THEY WON'T GET AWAY WITH THIS!

HUFF...
WHY...
AM I THE ONLY ONE...
CLUTCH
AM I THE ONLY ONE...
HOW?
WHY?!

MITSUKI'S THE ONLY ONE WHO FINDS HAPPINESS.
BUT NOT THIS TIME.
WOBBLE...
THE TWO OF THEM? TOGETHER? I WON'T ALLOW IT.
HELLO? IS THIS THE XX LAW FIRM?

I'M HOME.
WELCOME HOME.
THAT LOOKS GREAT.
I HAD TIME, SO I MADE A TON.
I NEVER KNEW YOU WERE SUCH A GOOD COOK.
WE ALWAYS ATE OUT ON DATES.
I NEVER REALLY HAD THE TIME TO COOK WHEN I WAS WORKING.
AFTER ALL THAT'S HAPPENED, FINDING THIS KIND OF PEACE FEELS LIKE A DREAM.
YEAH...

DING-DOOONG
ピンポーン
REGISTERED MAIL!
REGISTERED MAIL...? DID YOU TELL ANYONE WE LIVE HERE?
NO...
STAMP YOUR SIGNATURE HERE, PLEASE.
A COURT ORDER?
Special Delivery
○○Court (Civi

FLAP...
MITSUKI, WHAT IS IT?
TSUKIKO IS...
TAKING ME TO COURT.

Chapter 13

HALF A YEAR EARLIER.
I TOLD YOU, OVER AND OVER.
I TOLD YOU I WASN'T MITSUKI.
BUT YOU FORCED YOURSELF ON ME. YOU RAPED ME--

PLEASE... STOP!
MM...!

WHY DIDN'T YOU STOP? COULDN'T YOU SEE HOW SCARED I WAS?
I CAME OVER THAT NIGHT BECAUSE MITSUKI ASKED ME TO. SHE SAID SHE NEEDED TO TALK, SO I...I NEVER EVEN QUESTIONED IT.
HOW COULD I KNOW?! SHE NEVER EVEN MENTIONED BEING A TWIN.

I KNEW IT...!
MITSUKI KNEW THIS WOULD HAPPEN.
IT'S WHY SHE CALLED MURAMOTO OVER.
CLENCH
YOU KNOW, MURAMOTO-SAN...
IF I PRESSED CHARGES, YOU'D BE A CRIMINAL.
KLATTA

I'M SORRY!
I KNOW I'M BEING SELFISH, BUT THEY'RE GOING TO TRANSFER ME TO NEW YORK! IT COULD BE MY BIG BREAK, AND THIS...!
I'LL DO ANYTHING, ANYTHING AT ALL! JUST FORGIVE ME!
PLEASE. PLEASE DON'T TAKE ME TO COURT...
I DON'T CARE ABOUT YOUR WORK LIFE.
KLAK...
YOU SAID ANYTHING... RIGHT?
IN THAT CASE...

MAYBE YOU'LL HELP ME WITH MY PLAN.
I'LL TAKE A PICTURE WITH ME POSING AS MITSUKI...
AND SEND IT TO COWORKERS THROUGH-OUT HER COMPANY.
WHEN YOUR COLLEAGUES SEE IT, THEY'LL THINK MITSUKI'S HAVING AN AFFAIR WITH YOU. AM I RIGHT?
IT SHOULD CAUSE QUITE THE STIR AROUND THE OFFICE, ESPE-CIALLY COMING RIGHT AFTER EVERYONE GOT HER TACKY WEDDING INVITATIONS.
IF HER MATCHMAKER OF A BOSS FOUND OUT, SHE'D HAVE NO PLACE AT THE COMPANY.

EVEN MITSUKI MIGHT STUMBLE UNDER THAT.
HEE HEE HEE!
IN THAT AFTERMATH, WHY, YOU MIGHT EVEN BE ABLE TO INVITE HER ALONG WITH YOU TO NEW YORK.
YOU'RE DERANGED.
DERANGED?
ME?
SHE'S THE ONE WITH A FIANCÉ, BUT I HAVE TO PLAY HER ON DATES WITH HIM...
WHILE SHE SCREWS AROUND WITH OTHER GUYS.
IF I'M DERANGED, MITSUKI IS A STARK RAVING LUNATIC.

BUT... MITSUKI IS YOUR TWIN SISTER, RIGHT?
HOW CAN YOU SET HER UP LIKE THIS?
IT'S *BECAUSE* WE'RE SISTERS!
I NEVER SAY NO, AND SHE KNOWS IT. TAKES IT AS A FREE PASS.
COMPLETELY USES ME, OVER AND OVER!
EVERYONE AROUND US ONLY SAW **HER.** PARENTS. CLASSMATES. THEY ALWAYS SAW *MITSUKI.*
AND MITSUKI SHONE ALL THE BRIGHTER BY KEEPING HER DULL, QUIET DOUBLE AROUND!

BUT...
AKITO-SAN SAW ME. HE SAW ME.
"TSUKIKO." "MITSUKI." I'LL BE WHOEVER I NEED TO BE.
SO I'M GOING TO MARRY HIM.

IT ISN'T A BAD DEAL FOR YOU, EITHER. YOU GET TO TAKE MITSUKI TO NEW YORK WITH YOU, RIGHT?
AND WHAT, YOU LIVE THE REST OF YOUR LIFE AS MITSUKI?
SERIOUSLY? THAT'S WHAT YOU WANT?
NO ONE IS GOING TO MISS "TSUKIKO."

WITH MURAMOTO'S TESTIMONY...
CLENCH
I HAVE LEVER-AGE OVER MITSUKI, JUST IN CASE.
NOTHING CAN STOP ME NOW.
I'LL DO WHATEVER IT TAKES TO MARRY AKITO-SAN.

MITSUKI, WHAT IS IT?
AKITO-SAN...
TSUKIKO IS...
TAKING ME TO COURT.

I CAN'T BELIEVE SHE'S ACTUALLY PRESSING CHARGES--
I'LL TALK TO HER.
SOMEHOW, I'LL PERSUADE HER.
DON'T EVEN BOTHER.
WHP
THIS IS HOT AIR. SHE'S GOT NOTHING.

THAT NIGHT, I ONLY TEXTED MURAMOTO AND TOLD HIM I WAS WAITING AT MY PLACE.
THERE'S NO PROOF I ENTICED HIM TO RAPE HER.
HONESTLY, I DOUBT EVEN TSUKIKO THINKS I'D BE FOUND GUILTY.
SHE'S JUST SUING TO INTIMIDATE ME, TO LAY OUT TERMS TO WITHDRAW THE SUIT WHILE TRYING TO GET YOU TO COME BACK TO HER.
BUT...
IT'S ALL RIGHT.

I HAVE AN IDEA.

ピンポーン
DING-DOOONG
ガチャ
KA-CHAK
AKITO-SA--
AKITO-SAN!!

SORRY TO DISAPPOINT.
CAN I COME IN? YOU WOULDN'T WANT YOUR NEIGHBORS TO HEAR THIS.

I DON'T KNOW WHAT YOU CAME HERE FOR, BUT I'M NOT WITHDRAWING THE ALLEGA-TIONS.
THAT'S FINE. WHAT IF I CAN PUT THIS TO REST ONCE AND FOR ALL?
OR WE COULD SETTLE THIS IN COURT. I'M GAME.

I KNOW THAT YOU USED MURAMOTO AND HAD HIM RAPE ME!
I HAVE A VOICE RECORDING OF HIM TESTIFYING THAT YOU CALLED HIM THERE.
YOU THINK THAT'S PROOF OF ANYTHING?
I NEVER ONCE SAID "RAPE HER."
HELL, DO YOU THINK *I* THOUGHT HE WOULD?
HUH?!
YOU DON'T EXPECT ME TO BELIEVE THAT!

AKITO-SAN WILL SEE THE REAL YOU AT TRIAL.
IF HE DOES, HE'LL ABANDON YOU!
IS THAT YOUR GOAL?
POOR TSUKIKO.
AKITO-SAN KNOWS THE REAL ME. HE KNOWS ME *BONE DEEP.*

ぱしっ
SLAP
LIAR! YOU CAN'T FOOL ME ANY-MORE!
I SEE. THAT'S TOO BAD.
SORRY ABOUT YOUR BABY.
I DID WANT TO STOP YOU FROM DOING ANYTHING STUPID.

BUT IF THAT'S WHERE WE'RE AT, DON'T EXPECT ME TO BACK DOWN.
DO WHATEVER YOU WANT.
FLINCH
YOU'RE FULL OF SECRETS. BUT ME, I COULD TELL AKITO-SAN ABSOLUTELY ANYTHING.

REALLY?
THERE IS ONE THING HE DOESN'T KNOW YET, ISN'T THERE?
AND THAT'S WHO THE REAL FATHER OF YOUR BABY IS.

LET'S FIND OUT ONCE AND FOR ALL.
WE'LL DO A DNA TEST.
YOU ARE CONFIDENT IT'S AKITO-SAN'S, RIGHT?

GRIP
DON'T YOU WANT TO GET AKITO-SAN BACK?
THEN YOU BETTER CLEAR THIS MESS UP ASAP.
IF WE KNOW FOR SURE IT REALLY IS AKITO-SAN'S BABY...
THEN THERE'S NO NEED FOR TRIALS AND THE LIKE, RIGHT?
BECAUSE HE'S A GOOD GUY...
FWSH...
BUT...
IF IT GOES THE OTHER WAY...

IT'LL BE YOUR TURN TO LOSE EVERYTHING, TSUKIKO.

IT DOESN'T MATTER HOW KIND AKITO-SAN IS. YOU CAN'T EXPECT HIM TO RAISE ANOTHER MAN'S CHILD, CAN YOU?
AND KNOWING THAT CHILD DOESN'T BELONG TO YOUR BELOVED AKITO-SAN...
COULD YOU EVEN TRULY LOVE THAT CHILD?

I...I DON'T NEED A DNA TEST. I KNOW THIS CHILD IS AKITO-SAN'S!
USE WHATEVER TWISTED JUSTIFICA-TIONS YOU WANT.
IF I NEEDED TO, I COULD PROVE IT!
WHAT?
IF YOU WANT AKITO-SAN THAT BAD...
WHY NOT PROVE IT YOURSELF?

RIGHT?

Chapter 14

Kagami Law Firm
Lawyer Kagami Osamu
I'VE BEEN WAITING FOR YOU, KAMISHIRO MITSUKI-SAN.
PLEASE.

AND WHAT HAPPENED AFTER THAT?
I DID WHAT YOU SAID.
I DECIDED TO HAVE TSUKIKO AND AKITO-SAN MEET UP.
I SEE. THAT'S GOOD.
YOU'RE TSUKIKO'S LAWYER... IS IT REALLY ALL RIGHT FOR YOU TO DO THIS?

MY JOB IS TO KEEP MY CLIENTS HAPPY.
AND THIS CASE? IT NEVER STOOD A CHANCE.
PUT PLAINLY, SHE LOSES IF THIS GOES TO TRIAL.
I DON'T GET IT. WHY TAKE HER ON, THEN?
BECAUSE I WASN'T SURE WHAT SHE'D DO IF I TURNED HER DOWN. SHE WAS...WELL, DEAD SET MIGHT DESCRIBE IT.
I'M SURE THAT **YOU** ARE MORE THAN, *AH*, FAMILIAR WITH THAT...?

I...YES.
TSUKIKO-SAN'S GOAL IS TO WIN AKITO-SAN BACK.
SHE BELIEVES THE TRIAL WOULD BE AN EFFECTIVE WAY TO EXPOSE WHO YOU TRULY ARE AND OPEN AKITO-SAN'S EYES.
SO YOU SEE, THE NATURE OF THE CHARGES DON'T MATTER TO HER.
HOWEVER...

AS I TOLD HER, EVEN IF AKITO-SAN HEARS YOUR TESTIMONY...
HOW COULD HE NOT ALREADY KNOW YOU, MITSUKI-SAN?
WHAT IF THE TESTIMONY DOESN'T MATTER? WHAT IF HE DOESN'T COME BACK?
TO THINK HE'D DO ALL THIS AFTER ONLY HEARING TSUKIKO'S STORY...
WOULDN'T THAT MAKE IT ALL POINTLESS?
ALL OF THIS I SAID...
AND SHE WOULDN'T HEAR A WORD OF IT.

FIRST, CRYING.
I'D TRY THAT. OR PERHAPS SEDUCTION.
MAYBE THOSE WOULD CONVINCE HIM TO DROP THE SUIT.
NICE TO MEET YOU. I'M TSUKIKO-SAN'S LAWYER, KAGAMI.
BEFORE WE TALK...
I WOULD LIKE TO MAKE A PROPOSAL.
I SUSPECT IT MIGHT NOT BE A BAD DEAL FOR YOU.
BUT TO MY SURPRISE, HE WANTED ME TO STOP TSUKIKO.
AKITO-SAN KNOWS ALL ABOUT MY TRUE SELF.

I WAS AFRAID OF...HOW THINGS MIGHT GO, WHEN YOU CONFRONTED HER.
I'M GLAD IT ALL WENT WELL.
KLAK...
STILL, I CAN'T WRAP MY MIND AROUND IT.
WHY WOULD A BEAUTIFUL, CLEVER WOMAN LIKE YOURSELF...
SETTLE FOR A MAN LIKE THAT?

WHAT SORT OF MAN IS DULL ENOUGH TO FALL FOR SOME SITCOM TWIN SWITCHEROO INVOLVING HIS OWN BRIDE-TO-BE?
YOU DON'T NEED TO TELL ME THAT.
WHAT'S SO GREAT ABOUT A GUY LIKE THAT?
IF HE'D FIGURED IT OUT SOONER, THINGS WOULDN'T HAVE GOTTEN THIS BAD.
I KNOW.

BUT...
A MAN LIKE THAT...CAN HE REALLY MAKE YOU HAPPY?
WAIT...!
I AM ACTING STRANGE, HUH?
WANTING TO SEE YOU AGAIN SO SOON.
WHAT?
DON'T TELL ME...
WELL, IT WAS JUST...
MITSUKI, YOU BLEW MY MIND.
ASKING SOMEONE TO STAND IN FOR YOU IS BIZARRE!
I'M THE ONE WHO GOT PULLED INTO YOUR SIBLING SQUABBLE!

はっ
AH!
WHAT?
THIS MAN HAS NO INTENTION...
ARE YOU SAYING *YOU* COULD MAKE ME HAPPY?
OF UNDERSTANDING MY DECISION.
IF YOU'LL EXCUSE ME.

WHA--?
GRAB
MY, MY. DON'T RUN AWAY NOW.

I'D LIKE TO SPEND A LITTLE MORE TIME WITH YOU.
YANK
ぱっ
UGH, WHAT IS HIS DEAL?!

MITSUKI SAID SHE'D DEFINITELY LET ME SEE AKITO-SAN...
BUT WILL HE REALLY COME...?
WELCOME!
!
AKITO-SAN!

HI. BEEN A WHILE, HUH?
DID YOU COME BECAUSE MITSUKI TOLD YOU TO...?
NO MATTER HOW MANY TIMES I CALLED OR MESSAGED HIM...
HE IGNORED ME EVERY TIME.
YOU WANTED TO TALK. WHAT ABOUT?
AKITO-SAN, DO YOU...
KNOW WHAT MITSUKI'S TRULY LIKE?

SHE PUSHED YOU INTO BEING HER STAND-IN.
DURING THAT TIME, SHE CHEATED WITH ANOTHER GUY.
YEAH. I KNOW.

CLENCH...
YOU'RE KIDDING ME...
THERE'S NO WAY. I MEAN--
IF YOU KNOW, WHY ARE YOU WITH MITSUKI...?!
MITSUKI AND I HAVE SHOWN EACH OTHER WHO WE ARE AND ACCEPTED IT.
THAT'S WHY WE'RE STILL TOGETHER.

THERE ISN'T... YOU CAN'T...
CLENCH
WHAT IS THIS?!
KLATTA
I'M THE WOMAN MITSUKI USED AS A STAND-IN SO SHE COULD CHEAT!
HOW CAN YOU ACCEPT THAT, LET ALONE FORGIVE THAT?!

I'M SORRY...
THAT'S ALL I CAN OFFER YOU. I REALLY AM SORRY.
......
WHAT MITSUKI SAID...
SHE WAS...
RIGHT...
BA-THMP
BA-THMP

FWMP...
ストン...
ANYWAY, WHAT ABOUT THIS IMPORTANT CONVERSA-TION?
I TOLD YOU!
COME TO THE MEETING WITH MY FIANCE. HELP WITH WEDDING PLANNING!
TSUKIKO? IT'S ME.
CAN YOU COME OVER TO-NIGHT?
......
MITSUKI...

HE KNOWS EVERYTHING, AND HE STILL WANTS MITSUKI...?
HE REALLY LOVES HER THAT MUCH?
HOW COULD I BE HAPPY...
WITH A MAN LIKE THAT?
BUT IF YOU EVER NEED HELP, YOU CAN ASK...

HUH?
IF I EVER NEED HELP? WHAT'S ALL THIS?
IF HE WON'T MARRY ME, THOSE THOUGHTLESS WORDS...
ARE MEANING-LESS TO ME.
KLATTA...
ガタ…
ENOUGH.
HUH?

LET'S JUST...
END THIS HERE.

KA-CHAK...
Thank you very much.
BIP
BIP
BIP
BIP

I don't want anything to do with you, so I won't move forward with the suit.
IT'S REALLY OVER...
YEAH...
SHE GOT IT THROUGH HER HEAD QUICKER THAN I EXPECTED.
I THOUGHT SHE WOULD CAUSE MORE TROUBLE.

BUT GIVING BIRTH ALONE WILL BE DIFFICULT.
WE'LL NEED TO HELP HER IF WE CAN.
HELP HER...?!
WITH HOW ATTACHED SHE IS TO YOU? IF WE GET INVOLVED ANY MORE...
TSUKIKO'S JUST GOING TO SUFFER.
BUT SHE'S YOUR SISTER.
YOU CAN'T COMPLETELY CUT HER OUT, CAN YOU?

YOU'RE SO NICE...
AKITO-SAN.
MITSUKI?
SORRY. I'M GOING OUT FOR A BIT.
THIS ISN'T KINDNESS.
HE JUST DOESN'T WANT TO BE THE BAD GUY.
MY FEELINGS.
TSUKIKO'S FEELINGS.
HE DOESN'T UNDERSTAND A THING.

PIKON
Kagami
My apologies for earlier. I really would like to spend a bit more time with you.
CLENCH...
HELLO? WHERE ARE YOU NOW?

Kagami Law Firm
Lawyer Kagami Osamu
KA-CHAK...
ガチャ…
GOOD EVENING.
I WASN'T EXPECTING YOU TO DROP BY.
THERE'S NO WAY.

TSUKIKO MESSAGED ME TO SAY SHE'S DROPPING THE SUIT. I JUST CAME TO THANK YOU.
HE KNEW.
YOU'RE THE REASON WE WERE ABLE TO RESOLVE THINGS SO SEAMLESSLY, AFTER ALL.
HE KNEW I WOULD COME.
YOU COULD HAVE JUST CALLED, YOU KNOW. YET YOU CAME TO TELL ME IN PERSON...?

I DID.
I PREFER TO HANDLE THESE MATTERS IN PERSON.
SHFF...
ス…
YOU'RE A RATHER SPIRITED WOMAN, AREN'T YOU? INDOMINABLE, EVEN. IT'S NOVEL.

YEAH...I'M NOT THAT EASY.
OH?

<Revenge: Mrs. Wrong> 3 * End *

Kagami Osamu

The lawyer Tsukiko hired in order to take Mitsuki to court.

Born from a discussion with my editor about introducing another attractive guy. He's a hot guy archetype I've never done before, so drawing him was fun.

He's going to play a key part in the latter half of *Revenge: Mrs. Wrong,* so I hope you like him.

"Haruna-chan Will Take Anything"

The first one-shot I drew for *&Flower.* Haruna is pretty cute.

The story centers on a flighty girl who repeats romances where she is constantly swayed by the opinions of others. Will she ever be able to find her own love?

Its tone is a bit different than *Revenge*'s, but I hope you like it.

HARUNA-CHAN
WILL TAKE ANYTHING

ガヤ
BUSTLE
ガヤ
BUSTLE...
I'M SO GLAD THEY MOVED YOU TO OUR DEPARTMENT, AOYAMA-SAN.
I ALWAYS THOUGHT YOU WERE CUTE.
I NOTICED THAT YOU'VE ALWAYS HAD...
YOUR EYE ON ME.
HUH...?

BA-THMP
ドキューん
AOYAMA-SAN...
ぎゅ
GRIP
YOKOKAWA-KUUUN.
YOUR GIRLFRIEND'S LOOKING FOR YOU.

YOU WOULDN'T WANT HER TO FIND YOU LIKE THIS, RIGHT?
DASH
HARUNA!
GLARE
THIS AGAIN?! YOU PROMISED YOU'D STAY AWAY FROM THE GUYS WHO'RE ALREADY TAKEN!
GUESS YOU HAVEN'T CHANGED A BIT, HUH?!

N-NO! SATOU-SAN WAS BRAGGING ABOUT HER BOYFRIEND...
SO I JUST WANTED TO SEE WHAT SORT OF GUY HE WAS.
HE JUST STARTED TALKING TO ME.
STOP GIVING BEDROOM EYES TO GUYS WITH GIRLFRIENDS!
FOR REAL, GET IT TOGETHER!
JAB
DO YOU WANT TO CAUSE ANOTHER BLOWUP AND GET TRANSFERRED AGAIN?!
IF YOU GET SENT TO MANAGEMENT, THAT'S THE END OF THE LINE.
DO YOU UNDERSTAND?
AWW...
HE'S NOT WRONG.

MY NAME IS AOYAMA HARUNA...
AND DESPITE WORKING HERE FOR FIVE YEARS, I'VE BEEN TRANSFERRED SEVEN TIMES.
EVERY TIME, IT'S GUY TROUBLES.
WHA—?
YOU'RE DATING TAKAYAMA-SAN?
SH—!
KEEP IT DOWN.
HE'S SO SWEET WHEN WE'RE ALONE.
WHEN I HEAR OTHER PEOPLE TALK ABOUT THEIR LOVE LIVES, I GET CURIOUS.
I JUST HAVE TO FIND THE BOYFRIEND.
LITERALLY EVERY TIME
THE OTHER PERSON ASKS ME OUT.
WE GET TOGETHER.
THE GIRLS FIND OUT, EVERYTHING EXPLODES, I GET MOVED.
HOTEL
HOTEL
SHE'S THE WORST!
JUST UNBELIEVABLE!
BUT THERE WON'T BE A NEXT TIME...

HAAH...
I'M JUST ANOTHER SAILOR LOST ON THE SEAS OF LOVE...
YOU DON'T KNOW WHAT TRUE LOVE IS.
OH?
SHOULD I TEACH YOU HOW TO REALLY LOVE?
HUH?
NO WAY.
YOU JUST DON'T DO ANYTHING FOR ME, HAYATO.

WE STARTED AT THE SAME TIME! C'MON, I'M A POPULAR GUY!
AND WAY TOO OVER-CONFIDENT. NO THANKS.
SEE, THAT ATTITUDE IS ANOTHER THING--
AND YOU'RE SO LOUD, IT'S OBNOX-IOUS...
PKRK
!
TAP

—!
SHOVE
WHERE DID THAT COME FROM--?
I'VE MADE UP MY MIND.
YOU'RE GOING TO BE MINE.
HUH?!
SERIOUSLY, WHERE DID THAT COME FROM?!

OKADA-KUN! WANNA GRAB LUNCH?
SURE.
I WANNA GO TOO!
HAYATO IS REALLY POPULAR.
NICE AND SOCIABLE.
THAT'S EXACTLY WHY I'D RATHER NOT GET INVOLVED.
I DON'T WANT TO CATCH ANY ATTENTION AND START ANOTHER FIGHT.
HARUNA!
LET'S GO OUT TO LUNCH!
GEH!
NAH!
I'LL JUST HIT THE CONVENIENCE STORE.
DON'T BE STUPID!
WHY ARE YOU KEEPING YOUR DISTANCE FROM EVERYONE?
C'MON, LET'S GO!

WHAT SHOULD I GET?
THEIR OMURICE IS PHE-NOMENAL.
IT'S BEEN A WHILE SINCE I WENT TO LUNCH WITH ANYONE...
I'LL GET THE OMURICE!
ME TOO!
MADE UP YOUR MIND, HARUNA?
OH... WELL... I GUESS I'LL HAVE OMURICE TOO.
Menu
......
HERE YOU ARE.

THAT OMURICE LOOKS FANTASTIC!
TRADE WITH ME, HARUNA!
YOU LIKE KOROKKE RIGHT?
R- RIGHT.
THEN HERE.
YOU TWO ARE AWFUL COZY.
IS THAT HOW IT IS BETWEEN YOU?
WE'RE NOT...
IT'S NOT LIKE THAT!
HAYATO!
WHAT WAS THAT ABOUT?

HEY.
WHY'D YOU ORDER OMURICE IF YOU DON'T LIKE IT?
MAKE YOUR OWN CHOICES AND PICK WHAT YOU *LIKE* FOR ONCE.
......!
MAKE MY OWN CHOIC-ES...?
I'M NOT THAT CONFIDENT. I DON'T WANT TO MESS UP.
IT'S SO MUCH SAFER TO RELY ON A SUGGES-TION...
CLENCH...

DIRECTOR FUKUYAMA IS BACK FROM CHINA.
HE GOT A MAJOR CONTRACT THERE. WHAT A GUY!
HE'S AMAZING! I WISH THE DIRECTOR WOULD COME BACK FOR ME! ♡
HA! NO WAY!
HE'D NEVER. OH, AND HIS WIFE? TOTALLY A MODEL BACK IN THE DAY. GORGEOUS.
DIRECTOR FUKUYAMA.

YOU'RE AOYAMA, OUR RECENT TRANSFER FROM ACCOUNTING, RIGHT?
UHM... I FINISHED THAT RUSH SALES QUOTE FOR M CORP.
MY, YOU'RE FAST. THANK YOU.
THANK YOU VERY MUCH.
I'LL DO WHATEVER I CAN TO HELP YOU OUT.
I HAVE HIGH HOPES FOR YOU.
STARE—
ぽー

GRAB
A-O-YA-MA-SAN.
IF YOU'RE PROVIDING RUSH JOBS...?
IN USE
HEY, WHAT'S THE DEAL? WHY'D YOU BRING ME HERE ALL OF A SUDDEN?
IF I DON'T GIVE YOU A LITTLE TOUGH LOVE, YOU'LL NEVER SOLVE YOUR PERSONALITY FLAW.

HUH?
AGAIN...
I'M... GOING WEAK...
...!
WHAT...
IS THIS...?

GROUND YOURSELF. FEEL YOUR SENSES.
MY LIPS...MY TONGUE...
MY FIN-GERS CA-RESSING YOU...
IF THIS KEEPS UP, I'LL--
...!
I--
FEEL EVERYTHING.

AM I DOING IT FOR YOU NOW?
HEH...
!
BLUSH
THAT'S NOT LOVE! THIS IS TOTALLY DIFFERENT!
I DON'T WANT THIS!

UGH! THAT HAYATO!
KLAKA
KLAKA
KLAKA
BUT...I CAN STILL FEEL THE HEAT.
I CAN'T GET HAYATO OUT OF MY HEAD. THE WAY HE WAS...
I MEAN...SO ANNOYING! CAN'T STOP THINKING ABOUT IT!
THIS ISN'T LOVE OR ANYTHING.
KLAK
KLAK
KLAK
THERE'S A RUMOR GOING AROUND THAT YOU'RE DATING THAT AOYAMA GIRL...
OKADA-KUN.

HAYATO...?
DIDN'T YOU SAY YOU DIDN'T WANT A GIRLFRIEND?
YOU LIAR.
EH, SHE'S NOT MY GIRLFRIEND.
MUTTER...
ボソッ
YOU'RE MORE FORCEFUL THAN I THOUGHT.
SO I STILL HAVE A CHANCE.
WANNA GO OUT FOR A DRINK TONIGHT?
MM. CHOICES, CHOICES.

ズキューン
BA-THUMP—
WHAT...
IS THIS FEELING?
......!
HUFF...
はぁ

WHAM
HARUNA?
WHAT ARE YOU--?
STRIDE
STRIDE

ぶちゅーっ
KISS—
バタン!!
BA-TNK!!
HUFF...
NOT JEALOUS, ARE YOU?
OR DID YOU FALL FOR ME?
がばっ
FWUMP
!!

<Haruna-chan Will Take Anything> * End *

Revenge: Mrs. Wrong Volume 3 released without incident!
It's thanks to all of your support.
Thank you so much.

As Tsukiko's attachment to Akito intensified, a new character—lawyer Kagami—appeared, spinning the story off in an unexpected new direction.

Will Tsukiko find happiness? What will become of Mitsuki and Akito? You'll find out if you stay tuned for the fourth and final volume.

Sayo Momota

**Special thanks to my readers, editors, family, and friends.
I'm here because of all of you.**

IF YOU LIKE, PLEASE LET ME KNOW WHAT YOU THINK!!

〒101-8001
TOKYO-TO, CHIYODA-KU, HITOTSUBASHI, 2-3-1
SHOGAKUKAN CHEESE!
EDITORIAL DEPARTMENT

SAYO MOMOTA

I have Twitter.
Username: @momotasayo

I write back.

Lately, I've been into Naruto.

revenge

MRS. WRONG

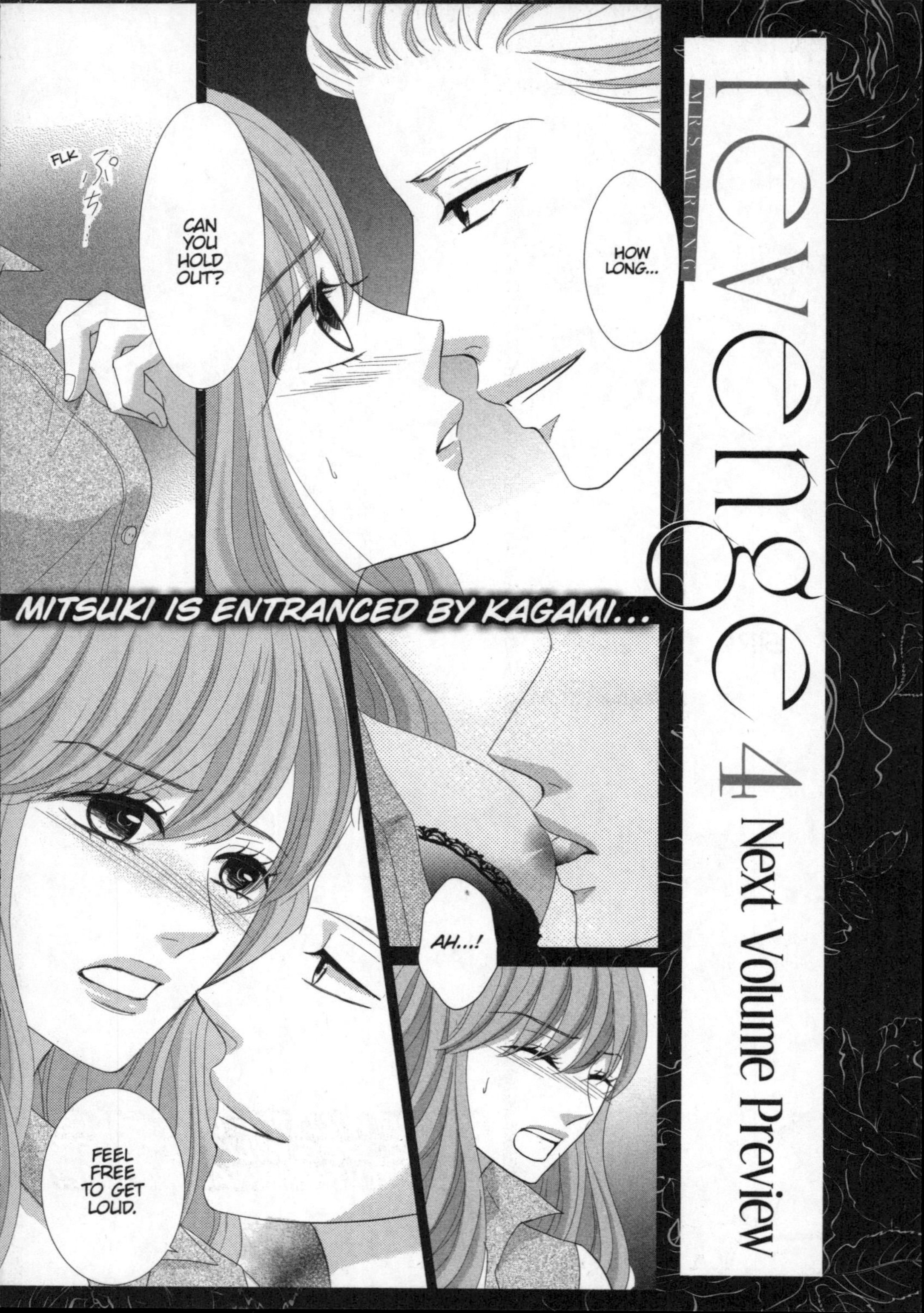

revenge 4 Next Volume Preview
MRS. WRONG
HOW LONG...
CAN YOU HOLD OUT?
FLK
ぷち…
MITSUKI IS ENTRANCED BY KAGAMI...
AH...!
FEEL FREE TO GET LOUD.

KAGAMI GOES TO SEE TSUKIKO...
SIR!
HELLO.
WHERE WILL THE DICE FALL?! YOUR EYES WILL BE GLUED TO THE FINAL VOLUME!
Vol. 4 coming soon!

revenge

MRS. WRONG

CLASSROOM OF THE ELITE
ART BY YUYU ICHINO
STORY BY SYOUGO KINUGASA
MANGA
1

1
Daily Report About My Witch Senpai

The Dragon Knight's Beloved
MANGA
1

Medamayaki
THE HAUNTED BOOKSTORE
Gateway to a Parallel Universe

Hello, Melancholic!
VOLUME 01
story & art by Yayoi Ohsawa

1
STORY AND ART BY Miyako Miyahara
I Can't Believe I Slept with You!

THE IDATEN DEITIES KNOW ONLY PEACE
STORY BY Amahara
ART BY coolkyousinnjya
1

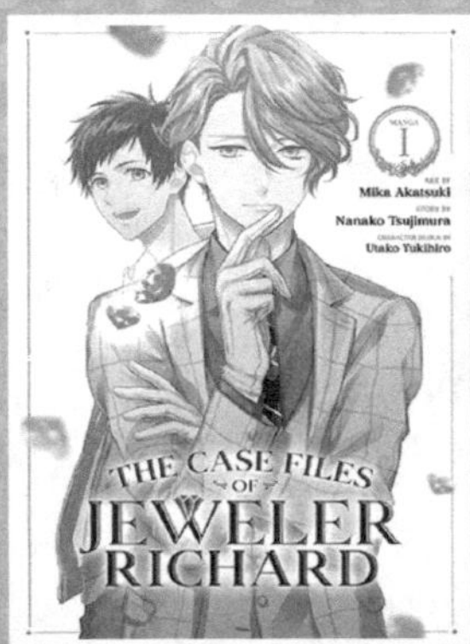
MANGA I
ART BY Mika Akatsuki
STORY BY Nanako Tsujimura
CHARACTER DESIGN BY Utako Yukihiro
THE CASE FILES OF JEWELER RICHARD

Magic Artisan Dahlia Wilts No More
1
Megumi Sumikawa
Hisaya Amagishi
Kei

revenge

MRS. WRONG

REVENGE -KAEDAMAKON- Vol. 3
by Sayo MOMOTA

Original Japanese edition published by SHOGAKUKAN.
English translation rights in the United States of America, Canada, the United Kingdom, Ireland, Australia and New Zealand arranged with SHOGAKUKAN through Tuttle-Mori Agency, Inc.

Translation: **Amber Tamosaitis**
Adaptation: **Matthew Birkenhauer**
Lettering: **Carl Vanstiphout**
Original Cover Design: **Nao SAKAMOTO (alpadesign)**
Logo Design: **H. Qi**
Cover Design: **M. A. Lewife**
Proofreader: **Danielle King**
Production Designer: **Christina McKenzie**
Editor: **Matthew Birkenhauer, Bambi Eloriaga-Amago**
Senior Editor: **Jenn Grunigen**

Seven Seas Entertainment, Inc. | President: **Jason DeAngelis** | Vice President: **Adam Arnold** Publisher: **Lianne Sentar** | Licensing Managers: **Y. Takahashi & Lena LeRay** | Editor-In-Chief: **Julie Davis** | Managing Editors: **Jack Sullivan & Shanti Whitesides** | Production Manager: **John Ramirez** | Assistant Production Manager: **Jinky Besa** | Prepress Technicians: **Salvador Chan Jr., Melanie Ujimori, & Jules Valera** | Digital Manager: **CK Russell** | Sales & Marketing Manager: **Lauren Hill** | Marketing Associate: **Leanna Cruz** | Administrative Associate: **Danya Adair** Inventory & Logistics Manager: **Marsha Reid**

ISBN: 979-8-88843-587-8
Printed in Canada
First Printing: August 2024
10 9 8 7 6 5 4 3 2 1